T0323359

Anglo-Saxon Myths

The Struggle for the Seven Kingdoms

Brice Stratford

Illustrated by Jesús Sotés

BATSFORD

First published in the United Kingdom in 2022 by
B.T. Batsford
43 Great Ormond Street
London WC1N 3HZ

An imprint of B.T. Batsford Holdings Ltd

ISBN: 9781849947664

A CIP catalogue record for this book is available from the
British Library.

10 9 8 7 6 5 4 3 2 1

Reproduction by Rival Colour Ltd, UK
Printed by Leo Paper Productions, China

This book can be ordered direct from the publisher at
www.batsfordbooks.com, or try your local bookshop.

Contents

Introduction

The Ealdspell is the ancient tale of England, of the Anglo-Saxons – it is infinite and ongoing, encompassing all there is to know and tell – every song and every story, every hero and every villain, every god and every monster.

It is the deepest lore, and sleeps unseen within the rest.

This book is a mere collection of fragments, surviving shards of the Ealdspell that, placed together, offer an interesting perspective. Some are presented as they were found, some in arrested decay, some rewilded, restored or propped up still against the straining remains of others.

The stories of the Ealdspell were usually sung, and almost always heard aloud rather than read. I have written this book with that in mind, and where the patterns and words might seem unwieldy or unfamiliar, try reading them aloud, to yourself or someone else. Explore the rhythm, the cadence, the musicality of the words, as well as their technical meaning.

I have invented nothing of what follows, only curated, interpreted, recorded and observed.

This book has been a labour of love, and this Ealdspell has brought me through strange times. I sincerely hope that you enjoy it, return to it, and retell the stories yourself.

Are you sitting comfortably?

Then I'll begin.

Scop

The Age of Gods

A scop is an Anglo-Saxon storyteller. The word comes from the verb 'scapan', or 'shapen' – to mold or to form – for it is stories that shape us, our past and our future. The scop would master old songs and sagas and retell them afresh, crafting new ones as they went along, and in so doing would shape the tribe or the court or the people to which they belonged – it is this that sets them apart from the 'gleemen', the wandering bards and minstrels of Anglo-Saxon England. Scops did not merely entertain (though this they did as well). Their narratives shaped and reshaped all who heard them, and their voice was forged and their tales were wrought with this in mind. For the Anglo-Saxons, to tell a story was literally to cast a spell, for this is what the word meant. The power of the scop was understood by all.

Moon over Middle Earth

In the beginning was the yawning void, the wet chaos of the chasm. And the abyss was of gods, and gods were of the abyss, and unmade chaos reigned.

In the wet and endless nothing of abyss, ice and fire met, and where they met was rupture, and there dwelt the fire in the water, and from the wet of that tireless flame, like a seed in the dark, there grew a root, and from that root there grew a leaf.

The leaf that grew had little to sustain it, and so it died.

And from that root there grew another leaf, and another.

And after they had died as well, and joined their mouldering siblings, a new leaf grew, and it fed on the rot of the others, and from that leaf there grew a tree, and from that tree grew seven worlds – six encircling one.

Highest on the tree was the High Earth, which one day would hold Neorxnawang, the heavens. Lowest on the tree was the Low Earth, which was fated to hold the halls of Helle. Between the two was the Middle Earth, and it is on this Middle Earth we dwell.

All stories have a beginning.

But each beginning is a thousand beginnings and a million ends, a single thread in an infinite tapestry.

Order from chaos, ice and fire – this is not one beginning, but many. The start of countless stories, countless worlds. Stories from long before we first took breath, stories still to come, and stories starting now.

This is one such story, and this is one such start.

From the branches of the World Tree grew many strange and different things, beyond the understanding of man, and the pain it suffers is eternal.

From the first roots of the World Tree the Wyrd were grown, who weave the fates of all, and weaved the tales we tell. The Wyrd is both singular and plural. Individual, triple and infinite. Wyrd is all.

The Wyrd first weaved Nerthus into existence, Mother of Earths, and who came into being pregnant with creation, birthing many things.

Mother Nerthus first birthed life to the High Earth, and then to the Low.

And on the High Earth, which was shining light, Mother Nerthus birthed a race of high gods.

And on the Low Earth, which was calm water, Mother Nerthus birthed a race of low gods.

And on the Middle Earth, which was both and neither, Mother Nerthus birthed herself, and then was Mother Erce, first of the middengods.

And those two sibling worlds of sibling gods grew – the high gods in the light, ruled over by their highest, whose name was Ingui – the low gods in their deep, dark depths of landless sea, the leader there unnamed.

But the low gods envied the light of the high, and the high gods disdained the wet of the low, and the sibling worlds invented war.

This first war was a terrible war. The worst and most destructive war that ever has been warred, and ever will be warred, until the last. The battle-pain was woeful, then, and this first war we call the Forewar, with Middle Earth the battlefield, and there shining Ingui was lost.

With much death and ancient pain, it was the high gods of the High Earth who triumphed, and the low gods of the Low Earth who did not.

This war took countless ages to be won, and when it was, the generation of the gods that reigned on high were led in war by one named Tiw, who we call Tue. Though older gods had flared and burned and disappeared like dying stars, this battle-closing victory belonged alone to Tue, greatest then in war.

We cannot know who led the low gods. After defeat they were gods no longer, undergods at best. Their memory obliterated, the dead parts of those who were killed became many other things, became stars and mountains, dwarves and monsters, seas and beasts and underkin.

When the great Low Army was broken, its soldiers and its offspring scattered about the seven worlds. Many of these creatures, these orphans and children of the Forewar, today we call ettins. Ettins defy easy description. They have many forms, and many types, and many still are *sui generis*, existing unprecedented, beautiful and terrible in their uniqueness.

Some have lived for countless lives and live on still, whilst others were born and thrived, and shrivelled and died, in the space of a human heartbeat. Some ettins built broods of their own, others kept immortal and constant, still more simply faded away.

Some are of the greatest power, nearer to the undergods they came from. Some have the strength of a hundred men. Some are nothing more than bestial rage, or the lowest cunning. Others have inhuman intelligence, plotting terrible, unthinkable things from their fens and their swamps.

Ettins are often cruel, and rarely to be trusted by man.

But ettins are only some of the many creatures we will meet on our exile through the Ealdspell. As the ettins came from the gods of the Low, so the ents came from the gods of the High.

From the spilled blood and broken parts of the High, many other things grew, and where the ettins were fed on pain and depth and darkness, the ents were fed on light, and came to know and learned to understand.

Ents are not as ettins; whereas each ettin is unlike the other, the ents are variants on a theme. Great and powerful things are ents, and old. Where ettins destroy, ents construct. Where ettins stand for chaos and for pain, ents are things of life and of care. What ettins take apart, ents hold together. This is not to say, of course, that ettins do not build and do not craft, but what they did was dark and strange, inverted and inward-facing. The things that ettins make from the wreckage of what has been cause deep and unseen pain, and cannot last, and run on spite – obscured reflections in a twisted mirror.

Both ettins and ents were amongst the things that populated Middle Earth after the Forewar, building towers and halls and strange shires, crafting treasures and armour and arms beyond our understanding. Some say that ents remain, still, though I have never known one.

Most common are the tales of ettins, many of whom you may have met before now, whether or not you realised.

This sums the first of life on Middle Earth, then, in the wake of the Forewar. The otherworlds we shall not speak of now. Much knowledge of them is lost to us, for today they are distant, and we have long forgotten the ways that lead to them.

Tue and the Binding of Helle

When war was won and the enemy scattered, Tue ordered the forces of the High Earth to search the World Tree, to round up and hunt down what survivors they could.

The high gods scoured the branches and combed the boughs and rummaged the fruits, and many were the things that were herded back to Low Earth, but many were the others that hid, and many were those that evaded capture, and started fresh stories of their own.

When the gods had done all they cared to, great Tue made Low Earth subject to the High, and bound the worst of the ettins and the direst of the dragons, the fresh terrors and the ancient undergods, deep into the very core of Low Earth – that boiling, drowned fire where they rage and burn still. This done, he took the heart of flame away with him, and bound the waters that made the world with bonds of ice that covered all, and could not break.

And the Low Earth then was a world of ice, and the ice became a cage.

Tue travelled thereafter from his hall, down, down the World Tree, through its spine, until he found its roots and visited the Wyrd, to whom all things are subject, and took to his knee and asked for counsel.

The Wyrd, when it spoke to Tue that day, did so in the form of three, each hooded. Each agreed to tell him of a single ettin still at large, and each assured him of their danger, and each assured him that the three would be the downfall of the gods. Though they would tell great Tue where each was to be found, none could be killed by him, try as he might.

Tue begged to be told what they would tell.

Wyrd told of the hidden woman, that she would be before his eyes unseen when deep and dark and wise. Wyrd told of Wearg, that he would in the Worldwood be, beneath the skies. Wyrd told of Wyrm, that it would dwell in chaos, far from land which earthen lies.

And Tue rushed forward to between the Wyrd and there, where nothing before had been, he found the hidden woman, and her power was inside hidden things, and once exposed Tue found no fight, and named her Seo Helle.

Seo Helle was strong and fine and was not to be killed, and as the deep, infernal hall of the Low Earth was now forever locked in ice, Tue bound her to the surface, and gave her Low Earth to rule as her domain, and made her jailor of her kin.

And Seo Helle was satisfied.

Tue travelled then to Middle Earth and to the Worldwood, and searched it long for thirty days and thirty nights, until he thought to travel to the moon, and watch from there and wait. And wait. And soon he heard Wearg's call, mournful to him, from deep within the spread of trees – and he gazed and gazed, and heard and heard until he found him, and down leapt Tue to face Wearg.

And Tue gave kindness, and flattery and food, and marvelled at the strength and size of Wearg, and told him that he had not captured him, for what would be the point? No bonds could hold tight such a one as he.

And Wearg agreed, and Wearg grew fat on food, and Wearg grew full on pride. Tue offered, then, to test his strength, to bind him, and to see how quickly he'd break free. But Wearg was wolf, and wolves know well of cunning-craft no matter what the trust, so Wearg accepted Tue for just as long as he was fed, and only for as long as Wearg could hold the hand that fed him, tight between his teeth.

With jaw-swords locked around Tue's wrist, hot breath upon his arm, Tue bound Wearg, and Wearg began to strain, and as he did the bonds cut tight and tighter still about his neck, and when Wearg realised he was tricked it was too late, and as his giant head became dissevered from his shoulder, Wearg bit the hand that fed him, as Tue had known he must.

Tue wrenched the mouth and pulled his stump away, and in his pain he bound the living head of Wearg to serve the Low Earth, and it became the Weargen mouth of Helle, and with no stomach left to fill was cursed with endless hunger, all-devouring.

Just one remained, and that was Wyrm.

So Tue, in weakened state, went far from home, and far beyond the realms in which his power lay and, maddened by his bitten wrist, Tue focused on his goal, let all else flow from out his mind.

The blood that swam from Tue thereafter filled the waves, alerted all to him and sapped his strength full well. Still Tue pushed on, anger-hot and pain-led.

When Tue found Wyrm, it knew that he was coming, and so swam on, and on, and led him up and down, and kept to the horizon of the horizon, to tire the one-hand even further.

And so, when Wyrm was in its territory and strong, and when great Tue was weariest and weak, Wyrm turned.

Its bite was poison, and water-chaos was its home.

Tue, who had won victory o'er all but still raged on for more, and weakened by winning again and again, did finally taste defeat.

And Wyrm bit Tue in twain, and swallowed both.

Wyrd measured out another thread.

Woden
and the
Wyrm

So Tue, weakened by winning again and again, did finally taste
defeat.

And Wyrm bit Tue in twain, and swallowed both.

And with Tue's power spent, that great and terrible Wyrm spread
forth from chaos and encircled all, and from it came such poisons and
such pain, that it was thought that none existed who could quell that
watery bane.

The high gods searched and scoured and rummaged the branches of the
World Tree for Tue, but all that they could find was blood in water.

Still they searched, leaderless and in vain.

Still they tried to fight Wyrm, but it was drunken then on Tue's power,
and wounds healed in an instant, and any weapon striking it was stuck
there fast, and wrenched from the attacker's hand. No god nor beast had
craft enough to fight it.

One god, who was the craftiest of gods, was Woden.

There are two kinds of intelligence, they say – the sort that stores facts
in itself, and the sort that knows where to find facts when it needs them.

Woden's was the latter.

So Woden travelled to Wyrd and asked for the knowledge that he
needed, of where Tue could be found, of how Tue could be saved, of
how he might defeat cruel Wyrm.

The Wyrd chose not to answer.

And Woden asked again, and begged, and still the Wyrd chose not
to answer.

And Woden rent himself and bled for them, and Wyrd declined – told
Woden that no matter how much blood he gave, no matter what the
sacrifice, they would not give the knowledge that he sought, and that no
other held it.

And Woden left the Wyrd, and wandered the World Tree. Sat down and
watched as Wyrm and water-chaos swelled. Watched the setting sun and
rising moon. Searched his mind for a route around his strictures.

And moons set, and suns rose.

Woden there, atop the World Tree, looked into nothingness and found
the way, and knew no knowledge given can compare to knowledge
found, and knowledge found cannot compare to knowledge taken, and
knowledge taken hard is knowledge earned, and knowledge wrought.

And Woden sacrificed himself unto himself, upon that tree, and hanged and pierced and nailed himself upon it.

As Woden hanged, undying, there upon the tree he saw and heard all things at once.

Woden, then, watched as a grey-brown bird perceived his pain, and begged to help. But Woden shook his head, and so the bird with sadness simply cleaned the blood that bled from him and flew away, and thus was stained. Woden named it Ruddock, and it became the bird we call a robin, and was blessed, but still had not a master.

As Woden hanged, undying, there upon the tree he felt and knew all things at once.

Woden, then, watched as a bright, white bird perceived his power, and begged to help. Woden nodded and said, 'Seek me the Wyrm,' and so the bird vowed service, and before it left it cleaned the unwashed filth off him with feather-towel and so, with black-stained middle, flew away. Woden named it Erne, then, and it became the bird we call a white-tailed eagle, and set to searching out the sea.

As Woden hanged, undying, there upon the tree he understood all things at once and there was blessed with madness, and so was visited by a pitch-black bird, who saw his perception, and begged to help. Woden nodded and took it in his hands, and let it die and be reborn as other things, and from it made his battle-women, who he named Waelcyrge, and sent these fighters far to seek out Erne and trap and hold Wyrm, and so they did, and with job done the dead and not-dead bird flew far. Woden named it Hraefn, and it became the bird that we call raven, and travelled then between the worlds.

And Woden joined.

And maddened Woden travelled through the shadow-land that was the land of death, and there he did see many, many things, which would have shattered minds still unembalmed by his insanity. Woden spoke with many of the things he met, and learned many of their secrets, and many of their ways. He was there for many lifetimes, and for none.

Woden, then, with what had been an instant and eternity, was Woden changed, unlocked.

Pulling at the noose that bound his neck, he tore himself from the Tree and stepped through madness into the self that was required, and in that

madness Woden saw things that had never yet been seen, and he took the blade of his mind and he carved them into being. Woden, then, invented the runes, and invented imagination, and art, and smuggled knowledge from beyond himself and to the worlds.

Understanding all things, then, Woden scoured the World Tree and gathered up nine herbs which grew upon it, first Mucgwyrt and Wegbrade, then Stune and Stiðe, Attorlaðe and Mægðe, Wergulu and Fille, and last of all found Finule. These are the nine that Woden sought.

Woden gave each herb a rune, and crafted each into a spear that he imbued with power.

In his madness, Woden brought these glory-twigs out to the chaos-sea, and to his Waelcyrge, who battled hard and long and hopelessly against Wyrm – for every wound that they inflicted instantly was healed, and every weapon they thrust in its hide was stuck there fast, absorbed into the beast.

But battle-frenzied Woden came, and sent the rest away, and roared to Wyrm to take him with its poisoned teeth, and Wyrm flew at him biting, but Woden leapt away.

Again he roared to Wyrm to take him, and again Wyrm charged, and again he leapt away.

A constant rage of taunt and dodge led Woden on Wyrm, faster and hotter – and soon Wyrm was angered and confused, and soon was tying up in knots, and soon it threw its snapping jaws at roaring Woden, and it felt flesh in its mouth and bit, bit hard, and felt a sear of pain.

Wyrm tried to open up its jaws, but it could not.

Wyrm tried to swim away, but it could not.

With Wyrm's mouth tight about its tail, stuck fast in the hide that could not heal for poison, Woden raised a glory-twig and thrust the spear into Wyrm, beneath its skull, and Wyrm hissed, and the spear stuck, and the herb prevented the wound from healing. Again and again, Woden plunged the spears into Wyrm, each herb anew – no chance at all for Wyrm to adapt, or to familiarise. Each spear became stuck fast, and the poison-craft of each did sear and spread the wound, whilst all Wyrm could do was strain, its tail trapped in its mouth.

As Woden watched, Wyrm began to pull itself apart. The weakened sections of the beast did tear and split, and soon the great and fearsome thing had pulled itself to pieces. Where once had been a mighty Wyrm there now were nine; diminished, helpless, writhing. The only jaws amongst them all were still blocked up with tail, which it could never swallow or spit out.

Woden seemed to grow, full mighty, and as he did so, Wyrm in segments seemed to shrink, and float encircled, minuscule, as swelling Woden let his mind infuse them all, and glory-twigs that now seemed like darts twirled clustered, tiny in his palms.

Woden scattered, then, the nine small segments. One to each world, one to the water-chaos above, and one to the water-chaos below. Woden alone knew where. Each there grew into a smaller, lesser wyrm, in time, and from their blood came many further, minor wyrms and nicors (which we today call knuckers, and which still were terrible and wild compared to men, but nothing to the gods).

When all had split and fled, from out the belly of the beast came Tue, bisected and in sorry state of cold unlife. Woden took him up then, dressed his stump, and bound him back together. He nurtured him with those nine herbs that there had struck and so enfeebled Wyrm.

When Tue was thus administered, the Waelcyrge carried him in comfort back to his hall in the High Earth. There he did rest, and did recuperate, and was cared for by his brethren. Tue did recover, through Woden's mad-craft, though was forever weakened by the ordeal, forever touched by death, and no longer led the gods of the High. His time had passed.

Now was the time of Woden.

Thunner, Dinne and Heofenfyr

With Wyrm defeated and Tue retired, still the Middle Earth was a ravaged world, and many nightmares amongst the offspring of the Forewar bided there still, and there were ettins and underwyrms, elves and dwarves, knuckers and thyrs, and much more besides.

So it was that the gods of the High Earth set about taming the Middle Earth once more, and banishing the children of the Low Earth back to their icy home, to dwell upon those frozen prison walls under the rule of Seo Helle.

The gods did battle, then, and skirmished long, and this aimless, general, useless effort brought small results. Woden decided to focus his force.

Woden first of all sent for Thunor, who we call Thunner.

Thunner was the biggest and the broadest of the gods; with a booming laugh and a bushy beard he towered over all, out-eating and out-drinking every guest at Woden's hall. No god did more to tame the Middle Earth than he, who rages still about the skies, for this was the task that Woden gave that day, this the mission. Thunner became his battler. From the core of that fire that once had warmed the Low Earth, a flaming axe was forged, and was called Heofenfyr, and always would return to the hand of he who threw it.

Thunner was given a great chariot too, called Dinne, which was drawn by oxen formed from the clay of the High Earth, from which living flesh could be cut to roast and eat, and always would regrow. Dinne could not be stopped when the oxen charged – not by any force, nor by any strength – and would always do as Thunner bid, whether he rode or no.

So, with great Dinne, Thunner thundered about the Middle Earth, striking with Heofenfyr at his enemies as he did, charging amongst them with his unstoppable ride, scattering foes, then slicing them down with his fiery axe, or simply leaping from his chariot and wrestling bare-handed.

The battles that Thunner waged on the giants, the ettins, the dragons and the rest could fill many books in themselves, though more tales are lost than can ever be found. It was Thunner's dance that did as much as anything to shape the Middle Earth to that we know today.

Thunner's work was long, and lasted much time, and last of the lands on Middle Earth he cleared was the Isle of Albion, fighting long and hard with that undergod Alebion who held it. When first they battled it was over water, treacherous and deep, which was a strength to Alebion and his brother, who battled side by side. Had either one been on their own, Thunner's task would not have overwhelmed him, but fighting them in tandem taxed his resources, for charging one left him open to the other, and hurling Heofenfyr at either left him sore exposed.

On the battle raged, and skies were black and roiling, waters boiled and spat. Thunner tired, then, of tactics, hurled himself uncaring straight towards the foe. When Alebion evaded him, Thunner focused on the brother, caring not for consequence, and as he hacked with flaming axe at face, Alebion crashed upon him like a wave, and Thunner then was blinded by the salt. Now only one opponent remained, but at the cost of Thunner's sight. He knelt there, then, over what was left of the brother he had slain, listening to the waves wap and wan, trying to determine how best to attack, and what ways were left to defend.

Thunner hurled his axe, but Alebion caught it in his depths – next instant Thunner was reeling, Alebion full force at him, then gone, then striking again, pulling back before the blinded god could catch the slightest grasp.

Thunner kneeled, panting, listening. He heard a new attack, too late, and still was knocked, and hard, by onslaught that he faced unseen.

He crouched, panting, mind firing, ears searching.

As Thunner prepared to die he heard a voice at his shoulder. It told him where to go, and Thunner obeyed.

The thunder god's terrible grip caught Alebion there, as he swirled in for a death-blow, and suddenly the slow and steady, merciless attacker was the panicked victim, splashing about for some escape from Thunner's brutal hands.

None could be found.

When the killing was done, Thunner heard the voice again, and it told him to open his eyes. There, his newfound friend bathed the salt-brine from them, and there restored his sight.

Before him was a tiny robin redbreast; Ruddock was his name.

Thunner thanked the bird heartily, swore that should he ever find himself in need again, he'd call upon the service of that reddened little Ruddock, who had braved the storm of wrestling gods.

With Alebion defeated, Thunner could set to work on clearing his erstwhile kingdom; the scouring of Albion there began.

Through the land, then, Thunner cleaved, and much battle there was, for much time. He dug deep rocks from earth to make his camp, near to a place today called Thursley. Here he returned, time and again, to feast on his oxen and take his ever-needed rest between the bouts.

With Alebion dead, the ettins and the undergods Thunner pursued focused mainly on evasion, though when caught they would battle ruthlessly. Often Thunner would track them over countless miles, and when he grew weary of killing with axe and chariot he would go unarmed and on foot, to better test himself, grappling and rolling in the fresh and still-young earth.

Ettins, though, are unpredictable prey, and many were insane. Thunner oft would wake from slumber to an attack, at which he would call his Heofenfyr to him and hope his reflexes were sharp enough to survive. On one occasion he was hacked at in his sleep by a particular foe named Deofol, whilst encamped near Thursley – the thing had found his axe, and tried to use it against its master, but Heofenfyr's flames extinguished, and at the moment just before the strike, loyal Heofenfyr's head did turn.

When Thunner woke to this, Deofol dropped the weapon and fled, leaping high across graves where Thunner had lain what remained of former ettins. As Thunner pursued, he dug into the ground, scooped up as much as he could hold, and hurled it at the enemy, knocking him flat, then raced to the final kill.

He tore at the earth there, searching for the buried escapee, and before he knew it up was down and down was up, and he was digging himself out from the very earth he searched through – in the distance, Deofol fled, having hurled the earth at him from out the very hole he'd made. They call the great hollow that was left there Deofol's Punchbowl, today, whilst the graves on which he sped are known as Deofol's Jumps, on the Hampshire edge of what now is Surrey.

Thunner spent a long time, then, tracking this quarry, and followed its trail up and down, round and about, eventually knowing enough of his enemy to set up a hide, and lay in wait. This he did at a hill today called Treyford.

For thirty hot days and thirty cold nights, Thunner lay in wait. Though ettin after ettin passed, and though each time they did, strong Thunner

hurled his Heofenfyr, and knocked them stony dead, still not a sign appeared of Deofol.

Finally, when five new graves surrounded Treyford Hill, Thunner saw him in the distance. Closer he got, and closer, and then when Thunner saw the yellow of his eyes, Heofenfyr flew. With a flicker Deofol was gone, and axe flew through the air as Deofol danced and capered 'cross the barrows of what had recently been his kin.

With a roar of frustration Thunner hurled a rock, which his target deftly avoided, cackling as he fled. The rock is still there, men say, and again, the ettin graves are known to all about as Deofol's Jumps.

The chase thereafter took Thunner and Deofol far about the land. In what now is Oxfordshire, at a place since named Taston, Thunner almost had him – hurled stone after stone as his foe ran circles about him, 'til Thunner dizzied himself with spinning and collapsed. The stones can still be found there, near to where he fell, by those that know how to look.

But once again, Deofol had escaped.

Thunner took to his chariot, then, and rode around the skies in hunt. Dinne, of course, was a loud and raucous ride, and all knew the thunder god came when he rode in it, and Deofol hid from him with ease. So Thunner called once more on Ruddock, and as the great god thundered round about the skies, making sure to be as raucous and as loud as possible to draw all ears and eyes, the tiny Ruddock red-breast flitted, unseen, to all the places that the god was not.

Ruddock soon found what he sought, and when he had he flew once more to the shoulder of Thunner and whispered in his ear that Deofol hid out upon a far peninsula, to the north, in what today is ceremonially Cheshire, and that he was aided in his rangings by the magic of a thyrs, which dwelt high in a certain cave set deep into a white and thrusting peak in what we now call Staffordshire.

So Thunner then rode Dinne across the Tree and to the otherworld of Fairy, Elfland, and there he had a harp made, paid for with the bones of things that he had slain. A harp it was, of elven-craft, cursed to fill the mind and to obsess the one that played it.

Thunner then returned to Middle Earth, and he clambered and he climbed, and he galloped and he clawed, until he found the cave of the thyrs, and at its entrance was a guardian, amorphous in the light.

The strange wight asked Thunner why he sought to enter, and Thunner told the guardian, truthfully, that he had brought a present for the mighty thyrs, a token of respect, and showed him then the shining elvish harp.

The gusting guardian was impressed. Thunner was given entry.

On he went, into the viscera of the cave, until he came upon the thyrs, and bowed.

'Oh great and craft-wise thyrs, in all due honour to your magic and to you, I here present a token of esteem – this fine and tricksy elven-harp, whose notes expand beyond the craft of any in the Middle Earth to play, even one with talent and ability such as yourself.'

'You underestimate me, clatterer,' the thyrs replied. 'My powers are beyond the ken of such as you. A harp's a simple thing to play, no matter what the gilding.'

'I did not mean offence, oh mighty thyrs, but even you could not play such a thing as this. There is no shame in it.'

'Of course I can, give it here.'

And Thunner did, and angrily the thyrs began to pluck, and then, confused, began to tune the instrument. 'Yes, I see. Interesting.' And the thyrs tried tightening a peg, and played with positions. Tried plucking and strumming, tried using a bow.

Thunner backed slowly out of the cave, but the thyrs didn't notice. Too lost was he in tinkering and fiddling.

Some say he still is to this day.

With that thyrs occupied, and his support withdrawn, Thunner then moved on to Deofol.

So the clatterer set Dinne to rage on through the skies about the south, far from the northern peninsula where Deofol did hide, which we now know as the Wirral.

On foot then, as the chariot thundered overhead, Thunner stealthily made his way towards the place, until at distance he spied the unsuspecting undergod, snoring away in the midst of the great hollow he had carved out from the earth, to sleep in comfort.

Thunner knew that to get any closer was to risk waking him, and when attack came it would have to be perfect. Heofenfyr's fire was extinguished still. Countless rocks had been thrown already, but none had struck, and all were avoided.

So Ruddock fanned the embers of Heofenfyr with his wings, and brought the flames of that loyal axe back to life, and Thunner delved, and Thunner heaved, and Thunner tore up the greatest chunk of sandstone he could find; huge it was, far, far beyond the largest thing he'd hurled thus far, and so expansive that no prey could dodge, with thyrs or without, if thrown correctly.

Thunner heaved the great red stone across his shoulders, hoicked it up and tossed it high, turning in the air, and watched as it came down. Just as Deofol's eyes began to open, and just as Deofol's senses whispered that something felt amiss – but before he could dance from danger again – Thunner threshed with the fiery axe, hitting Deofol hard in the head.

As he reeled from the blow, and Heofenfyr returned, right in the centre of that massive, plummeting rock was Deofol embedded, and right in the centre of that great earthen hollow was the bloated hunk of sandstone wedged, secure, immovable. Thunner then was sated, his prey caught, trapped beneath the monument.

Thunner rode in triumph then, wide across Albion, and drank good beer, and ate roasted ox, and slept a sound and satisfied sleep, in a place which he blessed thereafter, and which we call Thundersley, in Essex. Thunor's great Deofol-stone can be seen in the Wirral still, and the nearby village of Thurstaston named after it.

Thunner then became protector of the Middle Earth, and still when storms rage can Dinne be heard, charging hard in battles high with ettins and with undergods, with dragons and with gigans. Still when lightning strikes can Heofenfyr's arc of flame be seen in combat, and ever after Ruddock has been held in high esteem, and still braves storm to serve his master as he can, and nowhere is that Ruddock loved more than in England – as well he might be.

Frig
and the
Elven
King

E lves are ancient things, older far than man.
So old that we on instinct know them. I do not need to tell
you what an elf is, at its core. You already understand, even if
the details might be disagreed on.

Elves are beautiful, are bright and are shining things, beholden neither
to man nor to god, to high nor to low, to evil nor to good. Elves simply
are. Their otherworld of Fairy, or Elfland, predates our own, lying
always to the left of the Middle Earth, no matter how it's looked upon
or how approached.

But elves are not the only inhabitants of that land of Fairy, nor are
they as they used to be. When first their otherworld was formed, elves
were all that dwelled within it, and they held full dominion there. Elves
then were all of ageless and of timeless sorts, existing since before the
flames of any sun, and all upon that sinister land of darkness thus grew
pale and bright. No children, then, were on the elven-land. No mothers
and no fathers, either. Especially no mothers.

For in the oldest times, when first the elves existed on their earth, all
elves were male, and lacked the means of creation – Mother Nerthus
does not dwell in Fairy, and Erce and Eostre belong to Middle Earth
alone. In this way were they constant, but also were they pained. For
elves felt hunger that could not be sated, and loneliness beyond the
imaginings of mankind.

When the elven-burden grew too great to bear, the king sent crates of
elvish wine to the hall of Woden, of an unparalleled potency, sure to send
the gods to thick and dreamless sleep.

As the high gods snored, then, the king led a riding-force to march
upon the High Earth, and with cunning-craft and nets the elves bound
Frig, that great goddess, and took her with them back to Elfland.

When first she was released, fine Frig was wroth, and full of rage. She
stood and bellowed there, roared at the pride of any elven king who
thought that he could be her consort. Challenged him and any others
there who thought themselves of highest worth, who thought her waif
enough that she could e'er be satisfied by their pale elvish pleasure, she
who had known the love of gods and monsters. The elves were pained
and were diminished by her rage, and all of Elfland throbbed with it.

When she realised all about her wept, Frig stopped, and reconsidered.

Frig was not a wily god, like Woden – far more like Thunner, she, a thing of vigour and of passion. She led not with her mind but with her impulse, and thus was changeable and fickle. Many do, today, misunderstand her nature. Though her carnal drives are pure and wild and given sway, she is no mere goddess of sex. Likewise, though she revels in her widened hips and ripened womb, and breasts that swell with milk, she is no simple goddess of fertility, or motherhood.

Frig is a goddess of peak Womanhood. That prime of life that stretches from the bud of puberty, through and on to menopause. Each woman holds a trinity within herself, a triptych with a large and central panel – Frig is the goddess of that time of life that makes a woman feel a woman.

And as the elven-men about her wept she felt her anger wane, and asked them of their woe, and listened.

And as the pain of the elves was unfolded before her, Frig felt it all, and wept for them. She had been stolen, she now understood, not to be a sordid consort for the elven king, but to be a mother to a land of lonely children.

She took the elf-king, then, gentle in her hands, and kissed away his tears, and agreed to stay with him there in his sinister world, and to care for and mother his people, for a time.

And so she did.

She came to be loved by the haughty elves, and she in turn came to feel for them. For seven years she dwelt there, and when she knew her time would soon be through, on that strange earth, she found that she felt sorrow, and did regret that she must leave the people she had come to love.

She went then to the elven king, who had been as much a father to his people as she had been a mother, and she kissed him, and with the powers of the high she graced him, and lay with him there, and let her warmth fill him and give comfort, and ease the pain of Fairy.

Frig went about the Elfland then, and joined with all the elves who she had come to love, and in each joining they were blessed, and the emptiness inside was filled.

So it was that Frig became heavy with her children, birthing seven times seven daughters to the elves, each bright and shining with pale beauty. These were the first of the elf-maidens, and each of these daughters married elvish lords and each had seven daughters of their own, and each was different from the last, and each had seven daughters once again, who married elvish artisans and craftsmen, warriors and the wise.

And the elves knew fatherhood, and the elves learned that deepest love, and found their way to the highest peaks of joy and worth. So the elven-burden was lifted, and the ancient hole within them filled.

This, then, is how womanhood was brought to the elves. First by force (which caused more harm than good), then by pity (which could never last), and finally by love (which was eternal, though fleeting, and left them forever changed).

An old and crafty lot, the elves, by any measure, but little enough without their maidens.

When Frig returned to the High Earth and Woden saw what she had done, he grew sore envious, and hungered for creation. So it was, he sought out Mother Erce, and desired her to join with him, and was refused.

But Erce has a sister.

For after Mother Nerthus had birthed herself to the dry land of the Middle Earth, she birthed herself once more to that land which was given to water. This middengoddess of the drowned earth was named Geofon, and the waves were her domain.

Woden travelled round the Middle Earth, then, spurned by Erce, until he found the perfect tree, and this he carved to the shape of a man, and clothed it, and sang life into it.

This he did again, and then again, and then again.

He named them many names, his tree-men – Sceafa, Seaxneat, Geat, and more; Wecta, Baldag, Withelgeat; Withlag, Casser, Uinta. When each was made and fresh he placed it in the waters of the Middle Earth, to the middengoddess Geofon's embrace, and he joined with her there, and their union gave the tree-men life, and thereafter they did breath and live as other men, and did roam mighty round the Middle Earth, and do just as they must.

In this way, then, were the tribes born, and the lines of the Seven Kings established, who all today descend from Woden, as many elves descend from Frig.

It's likely you do, too.

The Burning Time of Waellende Wulf

D own, down in her frozen hall of the Low Earth, Seo Helle
grew restless.
No man can comprehend the mind of Seo Helle, can
understand her motivation, pick apart her impulse. She
rules her land with firmness and, whether through spite or duty, sadism
or pride, keeps her denizens ever bound to the Low, and spurs the
Hellemouth ever on to consume and to devour, to ever enrich her
realm with subjects.

Whether it was rebellion, or boredom, or simply because she was
feeling cold that day, no man can say, and no woman will let slip.
Nevertheless, this is the tale that unfolded.

On the Middle Earth then, in the vicinity of what we now call
Somerset, there lived a dragon by the name of Blawbaerne, so named
for the bright blue flame he breathed, hotter than the flame of any rival.
Blawbaerne was a child of the Forewar, but was not hostile by nature.
Like many others of his kind, he was content to keep himself to himself,
and live out what life he could in relative isolation, harmless. In this way
were many waifs and strays from the Low Earth allowed to carry on
throughout the Middle.

But Seo Helle knew well of him.

And Seo Helle knew well where he was found most days, lounging on
the mudflats of the Sumortunsaete, basking in the coolness of the waters
and the freshness of the air; not in many years had Blawbaerne's bright
blue flame a-burned.

And Seo Helle thought it a pity.

She came to him there, and with a stroke of his great tail she told him he
was fine, and Blawbaerne stretched out and enjoyed the stroking; and with
a scratch of his back she told him he was grand, and Blawbaerne preened
and posed, and he enjoyed the scratching; and with a caress of his chin
she told him he was glorious, and with a blissful sigh Blawbaerne let her.

In an instant she was there, bestride the foolish beast, atop him, with
an ettin-crafted harness round about his throat, and he roared in his
surprise, too late, and she reared and rode him up, and in his pain and
his confusion he obeyed, and could do little else.

Seo Helle rode him hard and rode him cruel that day, round about the
Middle Earth and beyond, and down and through until they reached her

halls, and with his bright blue fire, which burned hotter than any other, she rode Blawbaerne round and around the largest lands of the Low Earth, that great and frozen world, and set the ice aflame.

But only on one side.

For that flame – though it lost its bright, blue hue once it dwelt in ice and dulled to golden oranges and reds – was still ungodly hot, just as the frost preceding it was an ungodly cold. So Seo Helle left one half of the land in frozen state, and one half of the land in flame, and there between them was a gulley through which Helle rode, and smiled, for it was at her perfect temperature.

The flames that were ungodly, however, were not made to dwell in ice, and strange things happened where they did.

Though the deep and ancient prison-bonds of frost were far too permanent to thaw, even from the bluest of Blawbaerne's flames, and though the winter-cage of the undergods remained unbreached, the ice held many layers, many circles of the under-prison.

It was the outer circle which found itself in fire, and which then gave a home to flame, and which, in doing so, released some inmates.

Of the ettins and the things which found escape that day, many were destroyed in heat, and many were destroyed in ice. Some simply cowered where they were, too terrified to flee; others were content to dwell on Low Earth still, in slightly more amenable circumstance.

But not all.

Five-and-twenty dragons, in particular, each many times more dangerous than Blawbaerne, each fuelled by anger, rage and pain. Though their flames were not as hot, nor ever could be, the will that drove them made them deadlier by far.

The dragons flew from where they'd so long been, and set about the Middle Earth, and with their anger and their fire and with their pain, they set with hate and violence to unmake all that there was made, all that reminded them of that which was not theirs. And de-creation raged, and destruction was all.

There was another being then, from out the flames, who was released. Not a dragon, this, but a gigan; great and giant, powerful and strong; one whose name was Waellende Wulf.

The fire within this Waellende Wulf was greater far than that of any

dragon and, though he could not breathe it out, was greater far than the bluest of that Blawbaerne's flames. Waellende, though the heat within him raged, was not a slave to rage, and could control and wield himself with discipline and care, and this he did.

Waellende Wulf travelled then to the High Earth, to the hall of Woden, and there he took his knee and pledged his service, and offered there to take upon himself the task of tracking down the hard, destructive dragons rending at the Middle Earth below, and send them each and every one once more to Helle.

Woden was impressed with this great gigan, coming to his hall, pledging him his service.

'If you this thing can do, then you will have your freedom, and be celebrated here on high, and always have a place here, in my hall.'

So Waellende went from there, and to the Middle Earth, and sought the decreating dragons as they took apart the world, for they were not so difficult to find, and trumpeted their presence.

'You are my kin,' Waellende Wulf did howl, 'you need not reave. I understand the fire in you, for I as well have fought and lost, and I as well have suffered by it.'

'You are an enemy if you do not attack that which we hate,' a dragon screamed, and dove at him, though on the gigan went about his words.

'That which is built we must extend, and better if we may, but we have not the craft to build a world from scratch, and when this Middle Earth is flame what will be left but second Helle? What will we have but twice the prison?'

'Then all shall be the prisoners, Wulf, and all shall know the pain we know, and none will be above us.'

'You are no longer prisoners; you can be part of all which once you lacked.'

'You speak words of the enemy, but our words are fire, and now you will be counselled.'

And the dragons descended on Waellende Wulf.

But I have told already of the flame which burned in him. His was a private fire that was not endless-spewed to all about him, and that he would not let be panicked frenzy, and that he would not let have mastery of him. His was a fire that was a furnace.

And Waellende Wulf there stoked his fires, and felt the flame and heat of him rise high within, and felt that hotness fill his limbs and chest and mind, and felt it give him strength. And when his dragon-kin descended, raging hard to decimate he who was victim too of all they claimed to be, who careless swung at enemy and victim both the same, they who would destroy the world which offered him redemption, Waellende let the battle-fires burn bright in him, and leapt to combat.

Though dragons screamed their heat and dove, the fire in Waellende burned the hotter, and the cooler flame outside of him did not a thing to damage.

The fight erupted, then, and with his hands and nothing more did Waellende Wulf pluck dragons from the sky, and tear and rend at their devouring mouths, and rip their wings from off their selfish forms, and as he did the seething battle-heat within his chest burned all the brighter.

Where the flames of the dragons and of Helle were merely red and blazing gold, and where the hotter flame of Blawbaerne was an icy blue, so now the seething flame of Waellende Wulf shone white, and brightest of them all, and Waellende Wulf was battle-shining hard enough to blind and scorch the dragons there about him, and there they screamed in sightlessness, twisted, turned in the sky, and all were there unmade by Waellende Wulf, and not a dragon left alive.

When battle there was done, Waellende did collapse, for though he'd won the day his battle-shining, bright white flame had burned him up. He lay there, amongst the bits and pieces that were left of those that he was distant kin to, and he wept for the empty hopelessness of that battlefield, at the pointlessness of all the rage and the destruction, which had not had to be.

Hretha came to him, then. That warm goddess of triumph, fame and glory, who also is goddess of speed, so fast and fickle does she come and go. She kissed his brow and gave him favour, and soothed Waellende Wulf, and thanked and honoured him. When he was ready, Waelcyrge rode; took him from beyond his flesh and to the stars, and on from there to Woden's hall.

That Waellende Wulf sits in the highest honours still, feasting there and dressed in Woden's finest garments, made his finest son – redemption won, his shining battle-heat become a warming hearth of home.

Back on the Middle Earth, from what was left of all the scattered dragons grew lush greenery, and life from hate, and in time the scars and wounds of fire were all and fully healed.

And from the great and lifeless body of Waellende Wulf, the battle-shining flame of white still burned, and the middengoddess Geofon came forth with waters to extinguish it, and in so doing she drowned the burning flame, and joined with Waellende, and from that heat of fire in water, flesh cohered, and there was made a newborn boy, an entish son of gigan and of goddess, a boy who would grow up to build, who would construct anew, and would maintain that which still stood, and would restore all that was lost.

And Woden named him Wada, and placed him in the seas of Albion for a crib, into his mother's arms.

And that land in Low Earth ever since has been half icy death and half a raging fire, and Seo Helle herself, who rides unending through her realm, is now half-blackened charcoal, half-ice white, frozen flesh; distorted by the ice and fire that should have killed her, so hard did it wreak upon her body.

And in a way it did.

But so strong was her binding, and so powerfully was she bound to the Low, that even death could not pull her away, and as it tried it merely pulled itself closer. And so it was, the shadow-land of death was dragged to the Low Earth, and joined with it, and they became one and the same. The Low Earth then was the product of its mistress, forged anew.

That's why we call it Helle.

Once she had tired of Blawbaerne he escaped his ride and, weakened by the cruel exertions, fled to what was left of the home that he had made. In his burned and broken hurry he misstepped, hurtling through the mud flats, desperate to cool of (and this at least he did). As he felt the cold and pitiless clay drag him down, and as he, trapped, was dying, he felt his flame go out, and did so happy. Men say his skull can be seen there still, and is a treasure of the Sumorsaete.

And Wada's story is another story, and Waellende's tale is ended.

The
Vessel
of
Death

Weary Tue returned, from rest in his retirement, down to the Wyrd, to ask if all he'd done was right, and all he'd given had been worth the loss.

They told him that he'd done as his Wyrd dictated, and that he'd worn the web of destiny well, and better far than most.

For though we each have Wyrd, the Wyrd does weave a flexible web, which can be bent in many different ways, and worn in many different fashions. We each must wear our Wyrd as best we can, and each must fold and stretch the web of it to best effect, for it cannot be broken, and it cannot be torn, and there is no cut but that which Wyrd provides.

With his work now done, the Wyrd did tell old Tue of three who he had fought and caught, of what their Wyrd dictated. Of the day when the gods would be exiled, forgotten by many. Of the Gloryfather, and the sacrifice of gods to gods, and Ingui's return. That the end of an age would begin at the crack of doom.

On that day, they told him, would the underwyrms rejoin the Wyrm. That Wyrm would surge and course to the Low Earth and Seo Helle would turn, betraying all, and unloose her forces on Middle Earth. The Hellemouth would regrow fresh body and new limb, break forth and vomit out its prisoners. The bonds of ice and fire would break, and undergods escape, and the Overwar would rage, and neither side would win.

And the Wyrd told Tue of a strange and terrible thing, which dwells within the Middle Earth, in a place that is both water and land, surrounded by a mountain, on which is built a high and golden wall.

Hidden forces, generations old, will guard this monster zealously for thrice thirty thousand years, until the time of men does wane. When the many guardsmen all are bones and rust to north and south, the seas around will freeze, and it will tear at its mighty chains.

This thing it has four heads like human men, none facing in a shared direction, each oblivious to the rest. One screeches wordless, ever mournful; one laments only sorrow; one sings wondrous music; one is silent, though some men say it whispers to them. Not one can hear or see the other, for each is focused only on itself.

Its great and spreading wings are like a vulture's, or an eagle's, and sit upon a huge and bloated body like a whale. Its legs are like the griffin, talons at the front, lion claws at back.

It spends its days from now until the end, writhing restless, ever beating at its fetters, swivelling eight eyes all about, tail straining, feet

kicking, talons clawing. Unending, tireless.

When the danger is long forgotten in a safe complacency, when the seas beneath are frozen and black trees grow, the crack of doom will sound and it will break its chains, and the Vasa Mortis will fly free about the Middle Earth, and the ending of men will be at hand.

And all will listen to but one of its four voices, and some will swear the Vasa Mortis sings of wondrous things in perfect, angel-voice. Some will hear it just lament its woes and will be overwhelmed with sentiment and empathy and pity for the thing, and will let all the world about them burn to right the wrongs it says that it has suffered. Some will hear its chanting, cawing rage, and all that they will know is anger. Some will say it whispers, but will not tell the things it says.

The four factions of humanity will not agree, and will not listen to each other, and will twist the words of the other three, to keep from understanding them. Each will call the other liars. Children will denounce parents, neighbour war on neighbour, and the son will be punished for the sins of the father.

No loyalty will live except the tribes which are the Vasa Mortis.

No nation, no family, no friendship.

In this Overwar much death and hate will deal, and there will be no mercy, and none will forgive, and all will be humiliation, shame, and hurt.

Discord and division will rule all.

And the Wyrd told Tue how Frig would die to kill the hidden Seo Helle. How Heofenfyr would freeze, Dinne be silenced, and Thunner die to kill Wyrm. The Wyrd told Tue of his final fight with the Weargen Hellemouth, of how he would be eaten once again, and kill it from within, and would triumphal die in doing so.

But Woden would not die, they said, and he would wander still, lost for a time to madness.

And from the wreckage of the worlds which there had been, a new time would grow, and new things would live which could not live before, and blossom from the corpse of what was past.

From Woden's madness would new knowledge grow.

A new time then would come, which would contain so many things that cannot be conceived of, and which were no concern of Tue's, and no concern of yours or mine.

And that are known to none but Wyrd, as well they might remain.

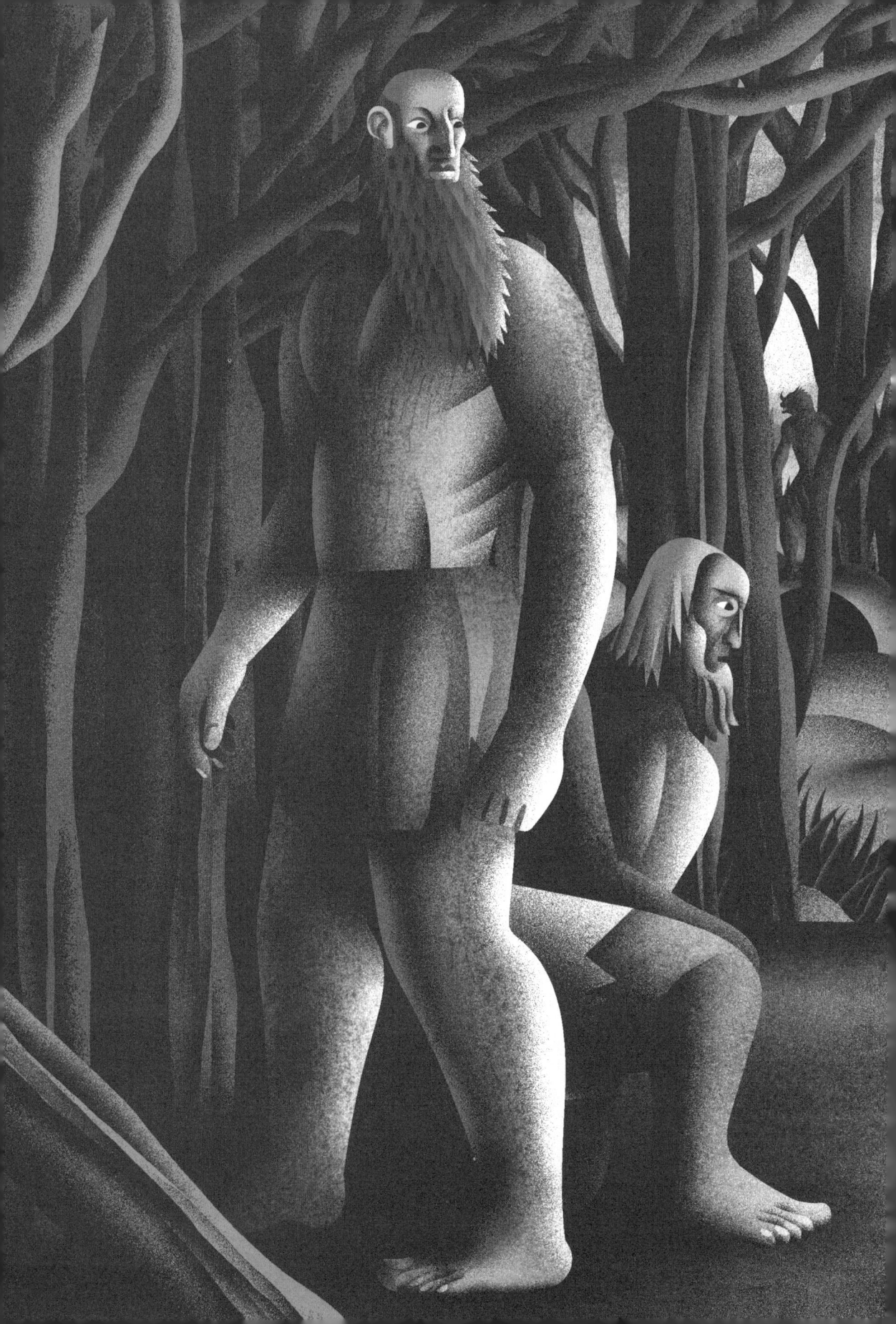

Wreccan

The Age
of Heroes

The wrecca is a wandering adventurer
– the Anglo-Saxon ronin, an ancient
knight-errant – banished to a noble,
meandering walkabout of derring-
do, seeking growth and the unknown. Turning
wreccan meant embarking on an exile of
discovery, a common formative or redemptive
path, especially for the warrior aristocracy. The
man who came back, if indeed he did come back,
was never the man who had left. It took as long
as it took, and the wrecca travelled as far as he
travelled, and gave his service to whoever needed
it. A rudderless hero, who gave his blade to
Wyrd for better or for worse, and went where the
journey took him.

Of Sheaf and Shield

All things must start, and always there is a first.

When the Middle Earth was reborn Geofon subsumed Erce and all for a time was water, as the Low Earth had been, and the water was bathed in light, as the High Earth was, and from the High Earth Woden gave his gift, and from beyond either Mother Nerthus birthed herself to Middle Earth once more, and was Eostre.

And an eagle flew on one side of the world, and a raven on the other, and both thought themselves utterly alone. And the waters between thought a speck into existence, and the speck thought itself into the wooden carving of a child, and the wood thought itself into a skiff, a skiff on which was piled strange weaponry, and on this bed of blades lay a baby boy, and beneath his head was a sheaf of corn.

And this baby boy, alone in all the world, thought sun and cloud above and saw it, and thought mountain and landscape and saw it, and thought of a people, and when his skiff had reached a shore the people he had thought of were there, and they raised him up and hailed him as their king, and they armed themselves with the weapons that he lay on, for they were a battle-mighty and a wandering people.

And from the wheatsheaf beneath his head grew field on field of food, and they learned to bake bread and brew beer, and no longer did they need to wander or to war to survive, and they learned to be still, and to grow, and to root. They named the boy Sceafa, and Sceafa grew as they did.

One day, Sceafa, still a child, was walking through the land which now was firm and solid beneath his feet.

As he walked, Sceafa came upon many things, and walked past many sights. He walked past a great tree, and he walked past a wide river, and he walked beneath a gaping sky, until he found in undergrowth the dusty bones of a long-forgotten man.

Sceafa crouched, and touched the blood-wood, and remembered the life that once it had led.

Before him there stood a grim and hooded man.

The old man put a rough palm gentle against the boy's smooth face, stared him in the eye, and let the madness of his gaze fill Sceafa.

With an intake of breath, Sceafa was alone once more.

After a moment of thought he took a bone, and from the ground beneath he took a flint, and he scratched and he hollowed and he carved, and he took up another bone, and more, and with his newfound instinct, with the mind that grew beneath his mind, he made an instrument.

On that instrument Sceafa played the first human music, and sang songs that began in hello and ended in goodbye, and told of a past that could never be returned to. His music filled and fed the minds of men, and blessed them with a taste of the madness that he had tasted from his father.

There grew the first blossomings of civilisation. There were tamed the beasts within, and so was given the divine to the monstrous. And so warriors were turned to farmers, and farmers turned to harpmen. So strength turned to prosperity, and prosperity grew to art.

Many years passed, and the songs that Sceafa sang and the music that he played grew as he did, and soon he was a man, and king of the people who were his.

And King Sceafa was a wise and otherworldy ruler, and thought beyond himself, and could see things that others could not, and could stare through time to envision worlds centuries apart, and could see the sounds and feel the notes to the tunes that connected them all.

Often would King Sceafa walk out, alone, through wood and over river, under hill and into dale, until he came to the hooded man with the wild eye. Sceafa would play, then, and sing such songs.

Time rolled on, as time has a tendency to do, and the threat of war returned to Sceafa's people.

Sceafa walked, then, and he walked, and he played and he played, until the hooded man came to him once more. Sceafa asked what he should do, and the rough palm went once again to his cheek, now bearded as a man's. The madness once more filled him, and with a gasp he was alone.

Sceafa, then, travelled to the fertile land. The ripest maid was found, and she was taken round about in her wagon, and garlands were strewn, and Sceafa joined with her, there in the field, and joined with Mother Erce.

When she gave birth to a baby boy, Sceafa gave his son the name of Scyld, and he took his mewling, newborn infant to the shore, and laid him on the wood of a great, round shield, and lit a candle at his head, and pushed his baby out to sea. He watched the flickering flame retreat as the waves took the child, and Geofon toyed with the tiny vessel, and the baby cried, and further it went from the shore, and further.

The light on the water paused. Floated there a moment.

Then it drifted back the way it had come, with a gurgled laugh as it returned to the stones at Sceafa's feet.

And Sceafa's people were protected then in battle, and lived to fight another day.

And Scyld grew up to be a man, and had a son, who he named Beowa.

Once more the threat of war came to the Sceafings. Once more Sceafa walked and Sceafa played, and once more was blessed with the mad-craft of his father.

And so, when Beowa was born, Sceafa took Scyld to the shore again, and he held him close and praised him, and touched a rough palm to his face, and held his gaze, and with his seax-knife he cut deep into the middle of his son, and held him as his legs buckled.

Scyld felt his blood join the water, then, and Sceafa laid his dying child onto the wood of that large, round shield once more, and placed the bloodied seax-knife at his feet, and lit the candle at his head, and pushed him from the shore.

Sceafa stood and watched the blaze of his son reach the horizon, watched the flame in the water.

Watched it disappear, as Geofon finally took her prize.

And the Sceafings once more were safe, and victorious in combat, and never again in Sceafa's reign would battle-threats return.

But soon enough the Sceafings found a drought upon them, and crops dried, and trees withered, and their people grew hungry. In dreams, then, Sceafa's hooded father came to him, and together in their frenzy they saw that which must be done.

And Sceafa took the baby Beowa to the barren fields, and with the clear-sight of madness in his eyes he took a scythe and reaped the child, and he sowed Mother Erce with the blood and the bone and the flesh of him.

The fields were ploughed then, and harrowed, and Beowa fed deep, and crops returned, and the Sceafings were well fed and bountiful once more. From the barleycorn that grew a special beer was made, which had been taught in dream to that mad-wise king. When he drank that beer he saw all things, did Sceafa, and understood much, and when the beer had passed he remembered fragments of his knowledge, and sang them.

In this way, the Sceafings swelled.

And time came and time passed and time carried on, and Sceafa was

old in his days, too old, and the Sceafings needed leadership anew, and Sceafa understood his time was done.

The old king went then to the fields, which throve as they did, and he reaped a sheaf of the Beowa corn. On he walked, deep to within his hall, and from a wooden box he took a seax-knife from the hoard that he had brought so long ago, ancient and entish and unlike any other seen. Sceafa gripped his bone-harp, then, and on it sang a song of age; a song of pain and of goodbye. He left the harp upon his throne. On he walked, and on he went to the armouries and found a freshly crafted shield, brightly painted, clean and smooth.

Sceafa took himself to the shore, and there was Mother Erce in flesh, older now, and there she stood before the Sceafings, and there they stood before a boat.

When Sceafa was aboard, he went to the centre of the ship and put down his sheaf for a pillow. He lay himself atop it, and as his people pushed the boat into the hands of Geofon he felt it heave and gently roil, and watched the sky above him going by in waves.

And this old man, alone in the world, thought moon and star above and saw it, and thought eagle and raven and saw them, and thought of a hooded father, a grandson and a son. He felt a rough palm on his cheek, then, and saw the clear and spreading gaze of his father's madness, and with the seax-knife he cut into the middle of himself, there atop the waves.

The bleeding king tossed the knife so it fell below his feet. He covered his wound with his shield. He lit the pyre on which he lay, and sang such songs. So Sceafa gave himself back to his father. Back to Middle Earth.

And the Sceafings from the shore watched the fire in the water, until they saw it no longer.

And in the fields, then, stood Beowa reborn, his beard thick now, full and long, his limbs full grown and strong, listening to his grandfather's voice on the waves, and knowing the tune full well. And Beowa sang such songs.

And Sceafa's heir took up his throne.

And the harp of the Sceafings was left to gather dust, and did so through the generations, until his great-great-grandson took it up in his hands when still a babe, and this babe was named Geat, and was the first to have craft enough in art to play that great song-tool since Sceafa himself, and when he did he felt the madness clear his eyes.

Geat grew from babe and he became a man, and often would he sing, and often would he play, and harp-craft gave him many things, and won him the love of his love, who was named Maethilde. His harp gave him fortune and glory, and he came to believe that all he could wish for, he could simply sing his way to.

Geat let the fields grow fallow, told his people not to till.

Geat let the arms grow rusten, told his soldiers not to train.

Geat played to them his music – his endless, perfect song, which kept them fat without the work of food, and kept them safe without the pain of fight, and kept them glued to him, in endless rest.

And the middengods grew angry at the insult.

So it was that Geofon, long left by Geat unbidden, rose up and took Maethilde, and drowned the life from her and held her tight beneath the waves, and kept her drink from the field.

So it was that Erce, long left by Geat unbidden, let the fields crack, and had no sympathy at cruelty of her kin, and would not intervene.

So it was that Eostre, long left by Geat unbidden, stayed far away, and left the Sceafings in unending winter, with no fresh life, no birth to bring them food or solace.

So it was that Geat fell back to all he knew, and all that he had left, which was his harp. Geat played and played, but still the fields were empty, still no water came, and still fresh life was held at bay. But as he knew no other thing, Geat simply played – could not begin to think that what he'd spent a life on wasn't all, could not allow himself to see that he had let things be ignored that could not be replaced, and never would be.

Geat played, and played such songs. His music had the power to lull Maethilde out from the icy grasp of Geofon, and this it did, but there its power ended. He had no craft to reinspire his love with life that she had lost, and had no craft to make his love his love once more.

And Geat cradled her wet corpse on the banks, and felt the depth of his heartbreak extend beyond sanity, tearing wide the doors of madness and flooding him with hard, unflinching sight. Geat cradled the harp of his ancestor, then, and with Maethilde's bones he refashioned it, and with her hair he made new strings, and from then on when he played his harp it was Maethilde who lived once more. With every song he played she breathed, and with every note he sang she sang to him, and Geat did not eat, and geat did not sleep, and Geat wasted away, devoted to his music, to his love, to his loss.

His people were ignored. War came. Defence did not.

And the Sceafings came to him, then, withered and sleepless about his instrument, and took him to the shore and placed him on a waiting boat; a blade beneath his feet, a sheaf beneath his head, his harp tight in his weary hands. The pyre was lit, and the Sceafings let Geofon, magnanimous, take her prize, long overdue.

And Geat sang such songs.

They watched it shrink, then, the flame in the water. Waited.

On another distant shore, a skiff reached land, piled high with arms and armour, and on this bed of blades lay another baby boy, and beneath his head a sheaf of corn.

And they named the baby Sceafa.

And civilisation spread.

Sigemund Victory-hand

Ages came and ages went, and men were born and men died, and much changed that cannot unchange, and much was lost that should not have been forgotten.

The Roman Empire needs no surplus words from my hoard.

Around two thousand years ago, in the waters of the Rhine, there sat a green and pleasant land; a fruitful, fertile island known by the Romans as the Insula Batavorum – the Island of the Batavi.

These Batavians were the fiercest and the bravest warriors of all the Germanic tribes that the Romans had conquered, and so were given status far beyond the rest, called upon for only the hardest of battles, in only the toughest of territories.

One such territory was Britannia, and one such Batavian was Sigemund.

Sigemund had been born of prophecy, and named as such, for his was the hand, so the hellerunes said, that would bear the greatest of victories, and win their homeland once more. A weighty prophecy, and one that had shaped him throughout his life.

Sigemund and his men soon found this realm of Britain welcoming, not unlike their own, and found their bodies and minds well-fitted to this damper climate, more so even than the tribes who dwelt already within.

Many tales tell how Batavian troops would, full in battle-dress, with not a sound, cross rivers fully armed – holding formation throughout.

At the Battle of Medway (AD 43), British tribes had camped uncaring by a river, knowing Romans could not cross in force without a bridge.

But the Roman had Batavians.

Swimming the river with ease, ranks held tight, Sigemund and the rest launched a surging attack and drove them back to the wetland of Thamesis. The Britons sped on and through in their retreat, knowing the land as they knew themselves, knowing well where firm ground lay beneath the wet, and where the easy passages were found.

The Romans tried and failed to follow, stuck in mud and muck, slowed. Foreigners to the land.

The Batavians, however, knew by instinct – they crossed as deftly as the British tribes and forced a confrontation, taking triumph there and glory, with Hretha singing loud and fierce, grappling the day.

That Sigemund then won much renown – though known already was his hand of victory. Caligula, the former emperor, had long ago awarded him the greatest honour that he knew to give – that of Roman citizenship. So it was that Sigemund, throughout the Roman Empire, was known by his Latin name, of Gaius Julius Civilis.

With triumph won and Hretha fed at Medway, Sigemund was gifted a cohort of his own to lead, and with his brother by his side fought many battles, and did much service for the Roman rule of Britain.

But no tide stays the course forever, and there is no wind that blows eternal, and the only constant in life is change.

In time, Sigemund grew to understand the British tribes as he understood himself, and as he understood his soldiers, and as he understood the land they shared. Sigemund's kin came to join him then in Britain, and joined with Britons there, and found a home. He came, in time, to find that more bound Briton to Batavian, and Batavian to Briton, than ever could bind either one to Rome.

He came, in time, to care more for the health of Britannia than he ever had for the empire, and news reached Rome that his loyalty was divided.

When reports came, in AD 66, of a giant brood of ettins in the North that were decimating local tribes, and imperial orders were to simply let them be, and allow the gigans' bloody reign, Sigemund disobeyed. He led his Batavian battalion to battle there, with his young nephew-kin, Fitela, amongst them, now of age. Many giants they killed, and many Britons they saved in so doing.

Rome seethed.

The Batavi were called back immediately, leaving wives and children behind after more than twenty-five years rooted. On arrival, Sigemund, the Victory-hand they called Civilis, was put in chains and sent to trial. His brother, who was no Roman citizen, was executed there and then. Even his name was purged.

But fortune struck the Victory-hand, as often proves the case with those born into prophecy, and, whilst he was imprisoned, the Emperor Nero (then in power) was overthrown. His successor granted Sigemund pardon, sending him back to the Insula Batavorum, where the Roman governor promptly rearrested and reimprisoned him.

With Nero dead, however, what had until so recently been strong and stable was, the Romans found, now soft and weak. The long-abused peoples of the empire were rising up, and revolution lit fires in the streets, and Sigemund saw his opportunity.

That which blunts some men merely serves to sharpen others, and Sigemund now was sharp as he had ever been, and he visited in secret

Weleta, the great and famous hellerune (or seeress), and she told him he would have his vengeance, told him he would have his victory, told him he would have and rule his home once more.

The prophecy of the Victory-hand was coming now to pass.

As civil war racked Rome in the summer of AD 69, and the chaotic Year of the Four Emperors swung full into sway, Sigemund led a revolt.

And the Batavian uprising was a bloody and a raging one, which united Germanic and Celtic tribes alike, as Sigemund had back in Britain, in a vicious and unbending army, sharp against the Roman rule.

He won independence for Batavia, and could have ruled as king.

Sigemund could, had steady mind prevailed, have taken the victory that was handed him.

But.

Whenever such a thought beat in his chest, so too did his *mod*. So too did the memory of his murdered brother, slaughtered like a beast for being less than Roman, and Sigemund felt the battle-heat of vengeance in him, and knew that he could know no peace.

The war raged, and many victories were won, and much damage caused to the Roman side, until, in AD 70, Hretha abandoned the Batavi as fast as she had come, and the inevitable defeat struck. The Batavians were once again brought to heel. The prophecy was broken. The Victory-hand was crushed. Sigemund had failed.

Sigemund turned wreccan.

He took to his noble exile, and, errant, wandered the lands – alone, unloved, despising of himself. With nothing left to lose, and no prophecy to guide him, our wrecca had many adventures, with Wyrd his only master, until his wanderings brought him back to the only home that was left for him, the home he'd known like no other.

Back to Britain.

And when Sigemund returned to the hills of Northumbria he found only rubble and ash. Blackened bones of friends and lovers strewn across the land. The homes that he had known could never now be known again.

The absence of the gigans there, slaughtered by Sigemund and his men, had loosed a greater danger, for it was those giants of the North that kept the dragons at bay, and the giants of the North (who could, if one knew how, be appeased and pacified) that kept the tribesmen safe, unwittingly, when they weren't killing them on purpose. For the realm of

Britain was and is a strange and well-established balance, and often that which looks to be an evil, something to be purged and carved from out the land, serves some forgotten purpose. Often those who seek to make things right revive, unknowing, long-forgotten wrongs.

Sigemund searched three days and nights, until finally he found a trail and followed it to survivors, huddled in the mountains, working for the dweargs (who we call dwarves) there in return for shelter, deep within their hillside caves. There amongst them, Sigemund found Fitela. He wept with joy, and looked into the still-young eyes and saw himself, and saw the future that this boy, his blood, could have – as yet untried, as yet unwasted.

Sigemund found his anger flame once more.

The survivors told him then their tale, and pointed to a black and flaming shape far off in the sky, which flew about an island eyrie. Sigemund saw it glitter on the water.

For with the gigans gone, one dragon in particular had grown in hunger and in boldness far enough to terrorise the land and grope for treasures, daily swooping in from its island lair – razing the settlements, flaming the crops, devouring the young.

And Sigemund saw that wreccan brought a second chance. Knew that here again was homeland of a different sort he could defend, here a people he could free from other tyranny, here a vengeance he could take that might, at last, be final.

And Sigemund had the dwarves shape him a blade, and forge him armour there anew, and swore that he would pay them well if he survived, and if he didn't then their craft was not worth paying for at all.

He swam, then, battle-full, towards the island, and he cared not for clouds of poison, jets of flame – ready to die, he threw himself to battle with this fire-wyrm as he had never yet thrown himself to battle before, and, as Waellende Wulf in ancient tales, he felt the shining-heat roar through his chest and outwards, and his strength became that of his ancestors', and his ferocity that of the land, and on the battle raged.

The dragon took him high, and Sigemund dragged him low. Sometimes in air they fought, sometimes in sea, which drowned the flame the dragon breathed, but almost drowned our Sigemund too, strong as he was in water.

Sigemund gasped for air on rocky shore, and down the dragon crushed for killing strike. As dragon dived, Sigemund hurled himself away, then thrust his blade through neck of beast so hard, so battle-hot, and dwarf-sharp as it was, it stuck through fast to rock, and pinned there that flame-serpent. With liquid fire rolling from its wounded neck and down its maw it started then to burn even itself, and with castrated hate the dragon there began its death moans, and started then to die.

And Sigemund left the wyrm to melt itself, and found the boats of others who, through many years, had tried and failed to fight the dragon, and found that dragon's hoard, that glittered in the water – filled boats with treasures and tied them one to another, and, as the flames took the island, swam back to Northumbria, pulling the bounty behind him as he did.

The Victory-hand found triumph anew that day, and found that even when prophecies are broken, still, they come to pass. That every man is bound by Wyrd, but no man wears it quite the same, and no man can predict the way it hangs, and much indeed can be made in the wearing.

Sigemund swam, then, heaving treasure, as the fire in water destroyed itself far behind, kept aflame unnaturally by burning fat of wyrm-corpse, until the island in entirety was lost, and Geofon took all.

With Hretha returned to him, Sigemund returned to the Northumbrian hills and founded there a tiny tribal kingdom, a homeland for he and Fitela to rule – for Batavian, Briton and dwarf alike.

And time burned on, as time always does, and the candle of life burned low, and Sigemund grew old and near to death.

And on this day the dwarves did carry Sigemund there, into the peaks that are today called the Simonside Hills, and there he met with Woden, who dressed him fresh in battle clothes and raised him up into his hall.

So Sigemund, ever rich in mod, sat high there ever since – gloried at the right-hand side of Woden, feasting in his hall. Dwells still within the hills, they say, as do the dwarves, safe in the eternity of legend, quaffing the potent, earthen beer they brew so well.

Those dweargs who in hillside reside today, are said to discombobulate, to attack and to distract the wanderers who seek that hidden door into the hillside, though they've been known (it's true) to join a toast with those adventurers who offer them a drink to memory of Sigemund – slayer of dragons, fighter of empires, defender of the North.

The Hand of Victory.

Heremod,
Hoarder
of Rings

I will tell you now of the mind of man – I have mentioned already the mod of Sigemund, and now shall explore what this means.

The mind does not reside in the brain, trapped in the skull as some believe, but sits instead within the chest – that great, locked hoard which holds the words and essence of a man. Within the chest there sits the *hyge*, the *ferhth*, the *hefa* and the *mod*. The first three do not concern us here. It is the latter, now, on which we dwell.

What is the 'mod'? It is a person's character and their awareness of that character. An understanding of one's own archetype, and of the obligations this brings – to the world about you, but also to the role you hold within that world. Commitment to playing the game; to serving the wider culture as and beyond your individual self; to living the art of life.

It is mod that takes you to the hall of Woden, and there dwell men and women who were enemies in life, and who did good and evil acts, but who were *modig* in all things, and played the part that they were given well, and did the needful, and shaped themselves well to their story and their Wyrd.

But mod can sour, and mod can stale, and mod can poison.

King Heremod had, in youth, the finest and most noble and warrior-like of mods. He was well-modig indeed, and won that kingship and the rule thereafter of his people. He had, of all the heroes, the highest renown amongst men, for the deeds of daring that decked his name.

Heremod's land was bountiful, his people strong and secure, well fed, fruitful and proud. The lands of their enemies looked up to and respected them, and those that hated Heremod did so out of fear and out of bitterness – none dared oppose or challenge his realm, and none could consider invasion. This was a golden time, of song and of music, of plenty and ease.

But Heremod aged, and the heart of Heremod grew slack in battle, and the hair that sat above his ears turned grey and white, and the hands that ended his weakened arms grew wrinkled and grew worn, and Heremod grew old, and Heremod gripped tighter.

Every woman, as we have said, is a trinity in and of herself. With age and life she merely unlocks new phases of being. A man has no such multitude within. He is destined to remain a weaker version of himself, and the only hope for him in age is wisdom, which few men now achieve, though more grow old than ever have before.

When Heremod grew old, no wisdom filled his bones to give him power, to counterbalance waning of his youth. When Heremod's hands grew worn he clung to every opportunity to desperately swing his sword. When Heremod's throat hung loose, he barked at those about him still with youth, or tried to convince them he was still as they, then lashed out as his swinging mood demanded.

The older and the weaker Heremod became, the more his sense of world turned inward, the more obsessed he grew with strength, with status, with respect. Every action now he took was driven by this need to be and seem and feel the younger, stronger, abler man that Heremod had been. Where he should have trained and built the younger thanes within his court, aided growth and given rings and power, Heremod merely competed, controlled, withheld.

Whilst the realms of his enemies stayed hungry and stayed hard, Heremod raised his young to be frivolous. When they asked how craft was done, how wars were fought, how food was farmed, they all were told not to worry, that they were too young for pressure and for knowledge, that there would be time enough for all of that. Play, children. Eat and sing.

Heremod came to consider himself a giant amongst the men he'd shrunken, pantomiming might and youth and telling all that he was towering and ageless. In time, he came to treat the vigorous, the talented and the young as weak (for he had let them fight no fights), as useless (for he had let them serve no purpose), as immature (for he had kept them from experience).

And Heremod called the strongest then about him, many of whom had served full well in battle, given and taken life after life for their king – his shoulder-comrades, companions at board. He bid these men, three generations' worth of warrior, to drink and feast, and feast and drink, and when they all were long in mead and incapacitated, had them slaughtered.

He would bear no rival, then. Could not stand to see the strength and youth he daily lacked. Had his throne raised ever higher, and the higher his throne the less he cared for those beneath him. The young were enslaved to the old then, and, instead of serving his people, instead of serving the future, Heremod forced the future to serve the fading present, and cannibalised the new generations to feed and bolster his own.

The young grew, unknowing and incapable, and, still young in mind, had children of their own, surviving on the charity of the old, who hoarded wealth, and lived alone now in great halls, whilst the youth raised families in makeshift hovels and borrowed shacks.

And the largest, loneliest hall of all belonged to Heremod.

In time, his bloated mod and aged obsessions overwhelmed the memory of his victories. With endless adolescence enforced on all who were younger than he – young minds unlearned in lessons of the past, young limbs untrained in inherited craft, young hands too soft to bear fresh swords – the kingdom of Heremod grew weak as he did.

But the lands of his enemies did not.

Other realms with wiser kings revived themselves, grew strong with wave on wave of ever-stronger youth. Passed over power, passed on wealth, enriched the future; the old sacrificed for the young, and not the other way around.

Heremod's enemies, built up over generations, rich in lineage and pride, attacked. Time and again, battle after battle, the withered, stale and insecure domain of Heremod was defeated. As war threatened the walls of his hall, the old man fled. Left his weak and war-soft people to their own devices, desperate to save himself at all expense, desperate to worship still the swollen and distorted mod that told him he was giant, told him he'd remake it all from scratch as if he were some god.

Heremod ran, then, as the hordes of war crashed down about his people. Wreccan, he hobbled over land and sea to find the realm of giants that would equal him, that would value him above and beyond those he had left, that would understand his greatness – the greatness that transcended age.

And in his homeland the people he had left behind could not farm, and could not war, and could do little else but sing and play. The enemy tore and reaved through town and homestead, and many were killed, and much was lost, and there was no song, and there was no food, and there was no hope.

Heremod came, in time, to the shores of Britain. To the forest kingdom of giants and ettins, the Ytene, and in his modness he presented his tiny, shrivelled self to those great, ancient gigans and demanded he be their ruler. The ettins plucked him from the ground, then, and saw him only for the nasty, wrinkled thing he was, and tore his gristled limbs apart, and ate him as he screamed.

Woden, then, once Heremod had died, re-dressed him in the clothes of youth, and Heremod that once had been was Heremod restored once more – modig and strong, generous and good. He wept for his people then, and for his folly, and was brought to Woden's hall and given a place at the god's left hand, his sinister, as great Sigemund had at his right – for good or bad, each ever had well served his mod.

And in that land where Heremod had reigned, to that battered, scared and placeless people, Woden gifted insight, and let them dream of battle-knowledge.

So it was that the survivors went to the shore, to plead for hope, for help, for anything.

They saw then, distant in the water, flame. And the fire drew closer, and was a candle, nearly but not quite burned out. And on the skiff there was a shield, and on the shield there was a baby boy, with a scar that seemed older than he was. Beneath his head was a sheaf of corn, and about him were treasures laid, and weapons.

The boy they lifted from the skiff. The riches of the boat gave the kingdom enough to rebuild, the arms gave hope. The child gave something to defend. He grew in time to be protector, the shield of the kingdom.

They named him Scyld, for Scyld was his name, and in his perfect youth they found an antidote to the rot of selfish age, and they left their endless play and learned to live, and found the deeper worth of toil and craft and mastery, of things beyond themselves.

Scyld grew to be their king, and his descendants were ever after known as Scyldings, and traditions and power and rings, then, were something earned to pass on. The youngest thereafter were built and raised, as Scyld was from the skiff, taught power and status that they might lead the ones yet coming after, on and on through time, each generation shielding the one that came before, then passing the shield onward to the next.

And what was lost, was found again.

The mod of man is in the story that we leave behind, and endings count far more than our beginnings, though often the two are hard to tell apart.

Wada's Dream

And the lumpen mass of rock and chalk, clay and green, cleaved out from all the rest by that Alebion was Albion, and was our Britain, and would one day be England.

In the oldest days of Albion, as we have said, the land was filled with ettins and ents; with giants, pixies and hobs; with hobbits and elves and orcs and more. A repository for all the exiles of the seven worlds.

One such entish giant was Wada – born from the blaze of Waellende Wulf, and the wash of Geofon.

The great divide between the ettins and the ents is the divide between creation and destruction. Ents build and construct, protect and preserve. Ettins demolish and unmake, diminish and drag down. Wada of Waellende Wulf was entish, and Wada was a master builder, the greatest of all things to be.

Much of the land as we have it today exists as it does thanks to Wada's entish craft. As he grew from a clod of a babe, he learned by listening to the winds, and talking with the trees. Wada let the knowledge in his bones become unlocked, and forged himself a set of tools that none had seen or thought before. With each tool he made, he grew in skill and in experience – the process of crafting the tools was the training he needed to know how to use them.

The greatest was his hammer – as capable of the finest and the daintiest of details as it was of cracking mountains, raising hills. The hammer would respond to none but Wada and his wife, Belle, and each would set about their work on different ends of the island, closing tight their eyes and breathing deep a breath, and calling out their special call whenever hammer was required – whichever held it then would hurl it through the air, across the land, to be caught by the other.

Scaping a land is hard work, and each night they would sleep deep sleeps together, and dream high dreams of all that they would build.

In time Belle became pregnant, and their son they named Wade. A loustering babe, with an endless appetite, Wade would spend his days with his parents' giant cow, Annett, glugging straight from out the teat the rich, thick, endless milk – for he gnawed at Belle, and had an endless appetite, and powerful as she was she could not sate him alone.

To aid in putting Annett out to pasture, Wada built a causeway that would make the passage easy, cutting from the north down to the south, and crafted for the comfort of those great hooves. In quarrying road-rock, so the great Hole of Horcum came to be, and once the causeway was concluded Wada dropped the unused aggregate in one great pile, which we call Blakey Topping.

Wada knew he wanted more for Wade than yet he had to give, but dreamt of giving it all the same. He wanted his son to live beyond the Middle Earth alone, and so he built a great and arcing road and called it the Wade-ling's Street, or Watling Street. It ran across the land, and when it reached the point where the sun rose, it arced high from Middle Earth and beyond, and where it reached few can remember, but it is said it stretched across the Tree and on, to a sort of crossroads, where the wanderer could travel on to any world and any age – even those which have not yet occurred and likely never will. Some say this was the land of Dream.

Just as Wada and Belle, while working, would close their eyes and breathe a breath, and call out for the hammer, so too had they a special call to Wade – on hearing he would cease his suckling and call back in response. In this way his parents knew him to be well. They would call out, Wade would call back, and on they'd go about their work.

Day by day this did occur, until the day on which it didn't, and Belle called for their son and their son did not respond, and Wada called for their son and he did not reply, and both screamed for their son and not a soul did answer.

Belle dropped the rocks she was carrying in her skirts and ran to the place where she'd left him. Wada let the mighty hammer fall and ran to the place where Wade was last. Each arrived as the other did, and not a trace was left of son or cow, except some puddles of the thick and creamy milk.

They roared for Wade, shaking the hills and uprooting trees, desperate as they were for an answer. None came. Falling to their knees and beating the earth in desperation, making great gouges still to be seen, Belle noticed another splash of the thick, white milk across the ground. And another.

And Wada and Belle set to following the trail.

And on it led them, on, until they found their way to Watling Street, and followed there the puddles of spilt milk, Belle weeping as they did for fear of their lost child, and all that might have yet befallen him. Wada could not feel his fear, so dangerous it was, and so he made it anger and he freely raged.

Before them, Watling Street arced high into steps and rose from Middle Earth, and on they followed it, on towards the Dreamland, and far beyond the bounds of earth and air and water, and deep into the inken black of endlessness, where ice and chaos-fire threatened still, and unmade shards of worlds that never were fell ungrown from the boughs.

Up ahead, lolling on the solid stone of Watling Street, lay their son – gurgling happily beneath the great brown-and-white cow he had ridden all this way, his mouth filled with an udder from which flowed still the thick, white, life-filled milk.

With a cry of joy and fear, anger and relief, Belle snatched him up in her arms, and as she did the milk that he was supping sprayed across the black, staining it with dabblings of bright and milky white, which glowed and flickered there, so filled with life were they.

She held her son tight to her breast and wept, and her tears joined with the milken stains, and they throbbed still brighter there with life and grief and ecstasy, and Wada held them both tight in his arms and sent them singing back to Middle Earth.

For him, however, the journey home was harder far than journey out. For a cow will walk up a set of steps more readily than down, and Wada had to heave the hulking beast up on his own great shoulders, and totter gradually back the way he'd come, stopping regularly to right the heifer, and calm it when it struggled.

From that day forward, whilst his parents worked, Wade was bound to earth with Annett, fastened by a set of clever chains his father crafted, joined to the ring in Annett's nose, and which no amount of strength could break, and no tool could damage save for the hammer that made them.

Wade soon grew to loathe these strictures, to despise his bonds, and hunger there for freedom. Daily, Wade would grunt and strain and heave at those pitiless chains, until he collapsed exhausted, and glugged himself full of Annett's milk. When he had energy again he once more set to spending it. In this way Wade grew strong, and Wade grew mighty, but still the chains gave not an inch. And Wade grew crafty then.

And day followed day, and Wade would sup at Annett's teats and listen to his parents battering and clattering, and hammering and clamouring, and they would finish their toil and return to Wade, and unchain him and hug him and hold him, and eat hot stew and sleep beneath the sky, and dream their dreams of what would be. And Wade's resentment seethed.

And Wade waited.

And Wade waited.

And Wade waited, until the day when his mother at one end of the country closed her eyes, breathed her breath and called her special call to Wada for the hammer, and Wade was bang between the two. As the hammer flew through air Wade bit the teat of Annett and she reared, and he hurled himself up to the full length of his chain and lengthened limbs, and he caught that magic hammer, and he beat his bonds and freed himself, and laughed and danced at his cleverness and craft, and cackled and capered at destroying the handiwork of his father, and before he forgot he hurled the hammer back on its way.

But cleverness is cruel.

For Belle had made her special call for the hammer, and Wada had answered with his, and he had thrown and thought nothing of it. But Belle had waited. And Belle had waited. And when she had waited long enough she closed her eyes once more, sucked in the deepest of breaths, inflated her chest to call her special call again – and Wade's thrown hammer hit hard between her tight-shut eyes, and with a mighty ring caved in Belle's skull.

When Wada found his wife he wept, and clawed at the earth and swung at the air, and the grief was more than he knew how to bear, and so he turned it into anger, and he raged, and he wrecked and he ravaged that road he had built for his son, and he tore the stones from the sky, and he cut the pathway off from Middle Earth.

All that now remains is a stretch that covers part of England, and some fragments near the stains of milk and tears, deep in the black, which we call now the Milky Way.

Wade felt his world collapse, and coldness fill his still-young mind, and in his shame he sent himself to exile, turned ever-wreccan, and vowed to turn his hollow freedom to his curse, his punishment. He took the hammer, which still held his mother's blood, and with it wrought a boat, and the blood and the love and the life of Belle filled that craft.

Wade made the strangest of vessels, then, which had the power to grow and to extend, large and broad enough to carry any cargo, to hold there any crew, but also still could shrink itself so small that it could fit inside a pocket, or be worn upon Wade's foot as nothing but a sturdy boot.

Wade took the ship from off his foot and let it grow to hold him, and once he climbed inside he found it had a will all of its own, and it would take him always where he needed most to be, and in that way his freedom was the freedom to never know or to control his destination, as no man truly does, no matter what the freedom is he feels.

Wade bid farewell then to his broken father, who could not look him in the face, and that strange, fantastic boat took him to the sky, sailed over his parents' empty castle (some say Mulgrave, some say Pickering), over the tallest tower, and away, and away, and away. Wade simply let it.

Left behind, that Wada felt his rage boil over beyond his own defences, and break once more to grief, and he wept until he had no tears, and drank a river dry and wept until he could not stand, and fell asleep there, alone, beneath the stars – no hot stew, no warm hug. Neither ever again.

As he lay there, surrounded by the shards of the path that he had built, once, to make a dream come true that never now could be, high and far above, the salt tears of his dead love glowed with rich and life-filled milk, and out from Dreamland, then, there grew the dream of his great road.

And Wada dreamt his dream once more.

And in his dream he saw her, battering and clattering, hammering and clamouring, and they finished their toil and came to Wade, and hugged and held him, and ate hot stew and slept beneath the sky.

When he woke he was alone once more, and cold.

So Wada lived to sleep, then, and in dreams he heard her name, and saw that great, milky, tear-stained way spread through once more to Watling Street, and in dreams he walked through time and found the happy days once more, and found his Belle, and held her tight there with his son, who still he loved.

In dreams he has a dream, still, and in dreams they meet again.

The Wayfarer

Wade left his grieving father, left his home, let the soaring ship take him then where most he needed to be, o'er many countless seas.

Seas of water, seas of land and seas of sky; of blackness, of ice and of fire. And Wade named his boat Wingelock, which some call Guingelot, and always Wade was led by it, whether small and in his pocket, grown and thrust out before him, ridden across the waves, or worn on his flesh as a boot. And Wade's craft extended to many lands, and Wade fathered many different sons, led by his growing boat, to many different mothers.

Child Wade then became Wade Wǽfre, the restless wanderer, the wreccan wayfarer. Many years passed, and Wade learned many things and helped many people in many lands before he returned to the realm of his father. This wayfarer lived full many different lifetimes, as he was of entish blood, and never stopped his growing, still, in strength and breadth and height, and a powerful, mighty man was he, as strong as any, and stronger far than most.

They say his battle-shine could find such heat and brightness, that he had such power of arm and heft of mod, that like his grandfather before him Wade once slew a dragon, rent in two. I have heard tell of gigans and of ettins that he put to blade, and many more besides.

Though none could resist the sword in his right hand, Wade was a lover of peace, and ever its worthy champion. He grew to be the greatest of his age, which was a long one, and greater far than any of our own – an immovable rock in tempest, ignorant of nothing.

When finally Wade found Wingelock returning him to the familiar shores of Albion, it was in the final years of Roman rule, and to a small settlement of Angles (they of Anglo-Saxon fame), who had come to Britain with the Romans and been rewarded there with land, and this tribe was ruled by a man named Offa.

This Offa was a mighty king across the water. Tales tell that he was blind until his seventh year, and did conquer then, before he was a man, in battle most of his kingdom. He did not speak 'til he was thirty, and none of his age showed earlship more. With a single sword he spread his borders, in a redemptive duel against two men simultaneously, which won him rule of many lands, and saved the honour of his father, Wermund.

Offa the Anglo had, then, in the waning of this Roman rule, betook himself a Roman bride, and had been given by her family land in that Great Britain where they should live and prosper.

This young Roman wife, near peerless in her elf-bright beauty, was a haughty and an avaricious one. She was, in Offa's tongue, called Modthryth, named for the strength by which she understood her self, her mod; her right and value in the land.

As we have seen, the very modig can be good and bad and both, and very little changes them when they are. At their wedding her family marvelled at the wealth she then enjoyed from her new 'barbarian' husband, beheld the shining glory of her garments and her gold, and straightway were aglow with envy for the riches there of Offa. She revelled in their envy, and urged them then to go back to her homeland and tell of it, to raise an army that could come and share in all the spoils, for there was plenty still to go around.

The Roman Emperor, when such a report came from Modthryth's kin, considered that, as Rome was head of the world and mistress of all nations, England should stay fief instead of free.

So it was, that the declining, falling empire of the Romans sent a force to plunder Offa's outpost, for technically that land still was all theirs, why should they let another profit from it?

And Wingelock tilted its bows and rustled its rudder, and sped Wade back the way he'd come, so many years ago, and the wayfarer returned to his home, to defend there that mighty Offa and his Anglo tribe.

As defender and as friend Wade disembarked, that day, by what we now call Colchester – borne faster than the natural wind to that same shore that waited for assailants. He went to Offa, then, and though he knew not the threat, he knew that threat there still must be, so there and then the Anglish forces gathered in full strength, and there and then the Romans landed hard.

Modthryth grew angry at the bristling defence, and did not see why her emperor should not have what was his. She did not like this towering, muscled man called Wade who came and stoked a fire with Rome. She accused him, then, of accosting her (as oft she had with others in the past). Of gazing on her wantonly, and looking to arrange that Offa would be killed, so Wade might have his faring way with her. Modthryth there demanded Wade be put to death for such an insult, such a plot.

Offa was a wise man, however, and a patient one. He looked upon his wife and understood the way she was, and understood the fear and panic, the confusion of loyalties that had led to this.

'My love,' did Offa say, 'you must have been mistaken. When did this happen, for it has not happened here and now.' She answered that it took place soon after their wedding night – but Wade had been away in the far east until that morning. She answered that she was mistaken, that it was when she was in Rome, but Wade had not been there since long before her birth. She tried to answer yet again, but before she could, Wade took a knee to her.

'O Queen of Offa, mighty Modthryth, beautiful and fierce and aptly named. Thou art a noble mistress, and I offer you allegiance in the struggle here which you must face. For now you have the forces of your father on the shore, that threaten here the life of your dear husband, he that stands so tall amongst his peers. It is a hard and necessary choice you face, my queen, to choose between the land and family behind you, and the family and land that are ahead. But choose you must. Command me now which you will hold, and I shall defend them with my life, whosoe'er it be. Command me now to slaughter here myself, my queen, and that I shall.'

Modthryth paused. A lifetime that had taught her to mistrust and to manipulate had not prepared her for the honesty and loyalty of men who think in terms of oath and *dryht*. She placed the blade of beauty that she wielded down, and, not entirely knowing why, she looked Wade in the eye, and looked upon her Offa.

'It is my husband who I choose, and always will. I hold now to the house that's of my future son; I choose not my father's, which is past.'

So messengers were sent to Roman ships to offer peace. None was to be had. Wade dressed for battle, then, and with a hundred of the finest Anglo fighting-men he hied him to the Roman tents. All who saw him ride were struck with wonder, and to the emperor they announced the approach of a man of might, grey-haired, silk-clad, shining like unto the elves, gloried proudly by the gods. With him, there, some hundred knights – the best, it seemed, from all the quarters of the world.

In great alarm at these reports, the emperor stood mute as mighty

Wade appeared within their midst and asked, 'Is the coming of his imperial majesty peaceful?'

The emperor spat. 'What is that to thee, wayfarer, who never does abide at home? Is thine own coming peaceful? Thou who hunts cruel strife and murderous contention, all throughout the world?'

Then Wade, a man of staunchest heart and steadfast truth, gently did reply, 'Peaceful indeed, for innocence will always have the peace. I am as you say, indeed, strife-hunter, for, ever ready at the summons, I eagerly do track it out, and when I find it, do destroy with all my strength. I hate the makers of discord, and never shall be friend to them, unless they cease from wickedness.' With these words he left the tent and, joining those awaiting him without, saluted to the Romans and departed.

The Romans were afeard.

The hundred riders rode away, with Wade wayfaring at their head.

As on they rode, Wade felt atop his steed that old familiar pull in pocket of his shrunken Wingelock, slowly growing, leading him to some new quest. He bid his men ride on, and followed where his Wingelock led, and found himself in a darkling forest, eerie with the quiet, broken only by a gentle sobbing from amongst some thorns beneath the fruit trees.

Amongst the thorns he found a woman. Beautiful, young, richly dressed, but whose silks were torn, and gilding stained.

She wept alone, there, and pitiful. When Wade asked how she came to be, she told him of her dreadful tale. Of how her father was a Briton ruling what today is York. Of how her mother died, and on that day her father's gaze to her became a hungry one, of how he pawed at her, and took the door from off her chamber – tried to do things, time and again. When she had bitterly refused a final trespass, and fought him off, he ordered men to drag her to the forest, cut hands and feet from off her limbs, disfigure her pure beauty, then leave her to the beasts.

The men had taken her, but could not carry out their Yorkish king's commands, so cruel and sordid were they, and so perfect was her innocence and elf-shine. In spite of their mercy, she had no food, no friends, no hope.

Wade took her hand and lifted her upon his horse, then rode to join his men, and on to Offa. He gave her food and comfort, and left her secure as they planned their defence.

Wade placed King Offa, and all but five hundred of his men, in the middle of the city – a large and empty square. He himself, with his own hundred men, hastened then straightway to the gate that first would welcome enemy attack.

Wade put in command of the gate next to him a youth of highest rank, the king's nephew, Suanus by name, with the aforesaid five hundred hand-picked men. When the first wave of the Romans came, they avoided Wade in fear, and focused all their force upon young Suanus. He sustained with valour, however, and resisted with such resolution, that they strove to make up with quantity all that they were outmatched in quality.

At length, of their regiments, two were put to flight in disorder, and of the five hundred men of Suanus, two hundred there had fallen. Before the remainder could recover from their weariness, a fresh wave of five hundred Romans more crashed down upon them.

Suanus sent a man to Wade, desperate for reinforcement, but he was tersely told to fight on bravely. Suanus obeyed without protest, and rushed upon the Roman hordes berserk – bore him battle-shining to their midst, so that it seemed not like a conflict, but the flight of lambs from wolves, or hares from hounds.

Suanus raged on, forcing through beyond the gate, slaying them clear to their fourth line. Red with shame, however, at asking Wade for aid, Suanus counted his life cheap, and his mod was sore ashamed to return from the enemy. By his own death, he hoped to redeem the reproach of cowardice, until Wade, in pity, commanded him draw back.

Suanus, though modig was indeed, overrode the pull of mod and did obey, and left the gate and hastened through unto his king.

The enemy, then, like a great force of water at the breaking of a dam, rushed through the gate in hot pursuit, thinking all of Offa's forces spent and confident of triumph, 'til Offa met them bravely in the market-place, and there they dashed against the mighty rock of his resistance.

In the rear Wade made his play, and wheeled about and forced them on, through that same gate, and like a sharpened sickle through the reeds, he rushed through the heart of those unhappy wretches, leaving wide and bloody swathes where'er he went.

The Romans, caught hard in the trap, fell back and there were felled. Wade let them flee, and Offa did the same, as much a gift to his fair wife as knowledge that they had no longer any need to fight them. The

Romans, then, were granted peace, and in ships gifted by the king they carried their dead with them back to Rome for burial in shame.

The Romans left Britain, then, and never did return.

And Wade was toasted and was given glory, there, and feasting much was held in Offa's court.

That excellent and fiery queen of the people, Modthryth – who had in her own way caused all the slaughter – felt shame then at her acts, and understood the consequence of selfish avarice and pomp. She took a knee before her king and begged for his forgiveness, and Offa told her he had nothing to forgive, for she was who he'd chosen for his wife, and he had chosen all of her, and always would, and she had chosen him in turn, when knife was pushed to throat, and he believed she always would.

Before that day, no brave man of King Offa's hall, except the king himself, had dared to look upon her, for fear that he her enmity would earn, and see him clapped in chains and slaughtered there most cruel. From thereon in Modthryth was a peaceweaver between the men of Offa's court, and much beloved. Gold-adorned and elf-bright, she prospered there upon the throne, famous for her generosity, the joy she found in life, and the high esteem that she was held in by her people and her king, who was, as I have heard, the best of all mankind between the seas.

Wade feasted then with the waif who he had found and saved from the woods, and much merriment they had, and in time she became pregnant. He soon felt the call of Wingelock once more, though it pained him hard, and departed promising that he'd return as soon as he was able, and they together would raise their child.

But whilst Wade was abroad and fighting foreign enemy, at home there were enemies still. Word came to York's king of his daughter's survival, and of her newborn baby son, and so he sent his cruellest men to strike when she was weakest. They dragged her out to the forest, and in that self-same place where she'd met Wade, they hewed the feet from off her legs, the hands from off her wrist, the nose from off her face. They tore her baby boy in two, and left the meat in a pile for animals to feast on.

Wingelock, of course, was racing to the place, but though it sped through sea of sky it was too late. When Wade arrived and slaughtered the men, he could do nought for his love and his son but weep.

And Wade wept.

And he wept until he had no tears, and he wept until he could not stand, and he wept until a grim old man stood hooded before him. Wade watched, immobile, as silently the old man rejoined the hands and feet to her limbs. Restored her nose to her face. Wade watched as the man with the mad-craft in his eyes put his son back together again.

The girl was changed, however, and left that day to travel alone, and to kill her father, which she did under pretence of submission. She turned wreccan, then, herself, and her story is not mine to tell.

Wade took his second-chance son to the only place he knew, and grandfather Wada held him tight within his arms, and wept for love of him, and felt his dream blossom anew in his heart.

But Wade once more was called away, back to wheresoe'er his Wingelock would lead him.

Wada named the rejoined child after his own father, the man whose battle-shining flame had caused him to be born, and who had died that he might live.

That baby's name was Weyland.

Wade in
the Water

Every land, every culture, every tribe has a master smith – a strange and powerful man who transcends the divide between magic and the everyday. Whose abilities stretch far beyond the obvious, and who is both inherent cornerstone of his community, but also forever an outsider, separate from the rest, never entirely understood.

Our man is Weyland, and this is his story.

Just as Waellende Wulf had been the warrior, Wada the builder and Wade the wayfarer, so Weyland was the smith.

Weyland was raised by that great craftsman who had raised his father before him – and Wada had learned from raising and from failing Wade. Where he'd kept the wayfarer distant from his work, with Weyland he held him up close, and every swing of hammer, every shift of stone, everything he built he did so with his grandson there beside him, and taught him as he did so, and trained him in the entish crafts that still he was the master of.

Once Weyland had learned the craft of the ents, Wada took him to the Ettinwood, that Ytene, and had him trained in ettin-craft as well. This done, Weyland went to what today is Oxfordshire (though ceremonially is Berkshire still), and there did Wada build an earthen forge for him at that great passageway between the worlds, and at this smithy Weyland stayed, and he was visited at his grandfather's behest by the greatest smiths of all mankind – smiths of silver and of gold, of black metal and of white, of weapons and of tools. Weyland, but a child, outclassed them all, and hungrily devoured the knowledge that they had to give.

But still he wanted more.

Having mastered the crafts of ettins and ents, and all the crafts of men, he subsumed all within him – melded the three to something new and unfamiliar, and with this Weyland-craft he forged new tools that made new weapons, new armour, things which could not yet be used so fresh and so unheard they were.

Weyland's craft was not just practical, for brute practicality is as empty and as hollow as a stone to a skull, and not worthy of greatness. Weyland combined his inventions with a beauty hitherto unknown, a grace and elegance that elevated even the humblest and most primitive of tools into an artwork, a cherished piece to which any king, lord or god might aspire.

And Wada realised Weyland needed more.

So on they went and journeyed north, to an island north of Scotland which we call Orkney, and Wada strode amongst the waters, wading through with Weyland sat atop his shoulders, and took him then to meet the dwarves who dwelt in mountain there, the brothers who were masters of the dwarven crafts, and who agreed to take him as apprentice.

Dwarves are a suspicious sort at best of times, wary and untrusting of outsiders, but when they saw the overwhelming skill of this young child, and when they saw the unknown things that he did craft, they were gripped with twin urges, each equal in intensity.

First felt was jealousy and envy – for they were thought the greatest craftsmen, and greedily hoarded their skills. The astonishing work that flowed so fluidly from this young whelp did burn their pride.

Second felt was joy. At the power, at the sight of a fellow craftsman working at outstanding rate, at the pulsing potential of the boy, and all that they could help him to become, all that they could forge him into.

And all that he could give them in return.

So these dwarven brothers, having struggled with their dissonance, came to a conclusion and struck a deal with Wada. They would take young Weyland to apprentice for two years to the day – if Wada returned to the exact place at the exact time exactly two years hence, then Weyland would return with him. If he failed to appear, Weyland would be slave to dwarves thereafter, to be done with as they pleased.

Wada considered, knowing dwarves to be a tricksy breed, but finally concluded that what they offered the boy was worth the risk. He shook their minuscule hands as gently as he could, and left Weyland in their care.

And a month passed, and a season, and a year.

Wada waded through the waters once again and went to visit Weyland, and found him full of passion and of life, chatter spilling from him of the things that he had learned and the craft that he was crafting, and Wada then was happy to hear all, and as he listened to his grandson he smiled and he smiled until he thought his head would fall from his shoulders. After feasting and pleasure, Wada held Weyland tight in his embrace, bid him good luck and goodbye, and waded back to the mainland, and returned home to his work.

They would never again meet in waking.

A month passed, and a season, and then a couple more.

But Wada was no fool. He knew the dwarves would have some plot to keep him from appointment, through distraction or delay, and so he set off well in advance, when still he had three weeks to go until the necessary time, and on arrival set up camp there at the spot, and waited.

And waited.

And the dwarves knew he waited there, and the dwarves knew why, and the night before their meeting – when Wada snoozed and snored asleep, dreaming blissful dreams in which he told Belle all there was to tell of Weyland and how wonderful he was – those dwarven brothers crept to the mountains high above, and with their dark craft collapsed them onto Wada, killing him instantly, and burying him there where he lay. Just a single, giant toe was left sticking out once they were done.

The next day the dwarves brought Weyland forth, filled with excitement and eagerness to see his grandfather, to tell him all about his work, to show him all that he had learned. The dwarves had made him swear that he would take no handiwork away with him, but he had hidden about his person one small gift for his grandfather, and was eager to give it.

The dwarven brothers made a show of waiting, of humming, of hawing. Of checking the sun and tutting. Finally they agreed that Wada had not come, that their bargain was clear, and that Weyland now was theirs, to do with as they pleased. The dwarves stepped forward, and he saw in their eyes a strange and unfamiliar glint, and he found himself gazing upon beings unlike those he had worked for and trained under for two full years, and Weyland saw pure greed, and Weyland was afraid.

Backing away, one of the brothers lunged – in a flash Weyland had the hidden seax-knife that he'd made for Wada, carved an eye from out the dwarven face, and ran.

Weyland ran then, and ran, until he stumbled full force into something that should not have been there.

It was his grandfather's giant toe.

The dwarves closed in, with others too, and weaponry, and strong, cruel chains and fetters of high dwarven craft.

Weyland held the solitary seax-knife there before him, his back against the toe As the dwarven whips and chains began to swing, and the enemy advanced, and no escape remained, in flew Wingelock.

Wade charged then through the spiteful foe, and leapt with blade in daylight glinting, and the dwarves screamed and were cut down, and those that weren't did flee. Weyland ran and held his father tight, and Wade thanked Wingelock, once again, for taking him where he needed to be.

They mourned great Wada, then, and cursed the bones of the dwarves they'd killed.

Wade tied a rope about the giant toe, secured it then to Wingelock, and together Wade, Weyland and Wada sailed across the sea and sky, back to their home.

They buried that great Wada near Mulgrave Castle, by the barrow of his dearest Belle, and Wada's grave can still be visited today. That night, as they held their vigil, Weyland and Wade wept hard for that master builder, a better man than either of them, who'd done more to make this land than any. They ate hot stew in his honour, and drank good beer.

That night, as they slept about his grave, they both dreamt drunken, grieving dreams. Both saw that great and milky, tear-stained way spread through once more to Watling Street, and on they walked, and on, and they heard laughter and song up ahead, and there they found great Wada, who had died as he dreamt, and simply stayed in Dreamland, together with his beloved Belle. The two were blissful there together, and welcomed Wade and Weyland to their castle in the sky with such warmth and such love. The four of them rejoiced that night, and talked and talked, and laughed and sang in Dream, a family, together, for the first time.

But not at all for the last.

Weyland's Smithy

Wade stayed in England then, for a time, and got to know his son, and helped him in his grief. Wingelock let him, for this was where he needed most to be.

Weyland worked hard at his smithy, and inherited his grandfather's great hammer, which he called Wadasearu, and which he altered that it might be borne by those who were not gigan. There, deep within his barrow-forge, Weyland practised the hard-won dwarven craft, and let it merge and meld with his own, with that of ettin and of ent. Let it splice with the ways of man.

Weyland there became the greatest smith the Middle Earth has known. He remains so to this day. His fame spread, then, and his weapons and his armour and his jewellery and his rings spread too, throughout the Middle Earth. Much prized were they, and much glory was there in the name of Weyland.

But Weyland was a lonely man.

For though his works were glorious, and though he knew their value, and gave himself freely to the crafting of them, his life was nothing but his forge, his world no more than smithy. Wade, that greatest of wanderers, who knew full well the varied paths of the world and the pleasures that they had to offer, worried for his son, and wished that he would venture forth, to enjoy the hard-won fame and glory Hretha had bestowed on him – for it can vanish fast as it appears, as well he knew, and hay must be made whilst sun still shines.

One day, Wingelock agreed – that ship about Wade's foot did lead him to the smithy, and swell and scoop up Weyland, and off they sailed through the great sky-sea and down to water, about the world, and where and why they neither of them knew, 'til Wade did see a certain tree and spy a certain hill, and recognise the route, and with a kind, familiar smile he understood their journey. Weyland was to meet his brother.

For Wade had many adventures on his boat, and much was the craft that could be played on it, and to many different doors did Wingelock lead him, and widespread were the children of Wade. Though none are remembered so well as Weyland, the brother he met that day was rare too, and able. Aegil was his name, and with his bow and arrow he could pierce through any target, no matter what the distance, and well known and well respected was his name – though nothing was it, then or now, compared to Weyland's.

The men met, rejoiced and feasted, before Wingelock took their father back upon his wayfaring way. The brothers, then, lonely both, and hungry both for fellowship and brotherhood, had many wild adventures together, roaming the land – Aegil hunting their food and protecting them from enemies as they wandered, Weyland forging them comfort and welcome at every town and hall, crafting arms and armour, treasures and jewels, for any who cared to ask.

These two brothers painted strong their name across the Middle Earth, and much glee they had in doing so. But.

Such triumph and glory as Hretha grants can come and go as quickly as the strike of a sword, and just as quick can turn from hearth to hell. As Weyland's fame spread, and as his treasures spread, so too did their value, and so too did the greed of avaricious men.

There was a king named Nithad, then, who was a cruel and brutish man, who did not hold to any moral path save for to fill his appetites, which endless were, and never could be slaked. He hungered for Weyland's craft, and hungered for Weyland's treasures, and he scoured the Middle Earth and bought and stole and hoarded all he could, as much to keep them from the hands of others as to hold them in his own. Yet still he had a hunger.

Weyland, then, could not be bought – for if his great and peerless skill had earned him anything, it was the freedom to hold no master save his craft. This Nithad knew.

Where Nithad could not buy, he stole.

So Nithad in secret had the brothers gifted then with beer, sent to them in Wade's own name – a special, dwarven beer brought from the Simonside Hills, famed across the Middle Earth for potency. After much carousing, both fell to deep and pleasant sleep, and in their dreams they feasted on with Wada and with Belle, in that high castle of Dream.

Aegil woke first, and did so with a gnawing appetite, so off he went to hunt some birds to fill their table. As they watched him leave, the king's men who hid outside entered the brothers' rooms and carried the slumbering smith away.

When Weyland woke, he found himself in chains.

To earn his freedom, so Nithad decreed, Weyland must forge the greatest sword that ever had been wielded by a man – a sword as sharp as stars, as swift as wind, as light as moonbeams, and pitiless as the sun. A sword of such terrible beauty that men would beg to be slain by it. Craft this, King Nithad said, and you may walk from here a freed man.

So Weyland did.

There are many different accounts of the forging of Mimming, and too many refracting fragments of the Ealdspell to recount them all here. Many months, Weyland took, to craft the thing – and little work he did until the very end. Three blades, Weyland forged – each a peerless work of death and art, each unparalleled until the one that followed. Each, in turn, Weyland threw back to the forge and destroyed, remaking in the image of the next. Finally, the greatest sword of all that had been was plunged into the river, complete, and Mimming there was born.

But Nithad hungered still.

Nithad demanded a glittering helmet to match, so shining was the beauty of Mimming, and this Weyland provided – a helmet unlike any other seen, which made the wearer seem majestic, no matter how ugly he was without, and could absorb any blow, no matter the strength, and turn any blade, no matter how sharp.

But Nithad hungered still.

Nithad demanded a mail shirt to complete the set, for sword and helm alone were not enough to march to war. This Weyland made straightway – a shirt of finest ringmail, which draped and flattered any body that it wrapped around, and strengthened the muscles beneath it, and the harder it was hit the stronger it repelled, and it was matchless, then, and beautiful.

But Nithad hungered still.

Nithad demanded gloves and boots, and spears and axes, brooches and rings and countless other treasures, too numerous by far to name.

Weyland refused. Demanded freedom. Demanded his right to walk away.

Nithad had him thrown into a deep and dark and hollow dungeon, and there did Weyland dwell unfed amongst the snakes – no other company, no water but the moisture of the walls, no food but the vermin of the ground. Too low the ceiling was to stand, too narrow the walls to lie. Weyland huddled there, stout-hearted, dauntless.

In time, Weyland was ripped from the womb of Erce and thrown to floor before Nithad, who once more gave him his demand.

Once more, Weyland refused. Demanded freedom. Demanded his right to walk away.

Nithad had him tortured, then, most cruelly. His hands and arms were kept secured with silken rope to velvet cushion, as comfortable and cared for as any ancient king. The rest of him was not so lucky, and it was a shaking, bloody wreck of a man who cradled his perfect hands in the corner of his black and hollow cell, and waited and hoped for the day when Wingelock would bring his father to save him.

King Nithad had a daughter, as beautiful as any brooch of Weyland's craft. Her name was Beadohild, and in her the cruelty and spite of her father was inherited as care and kindness. She came to Weyland, then, and nursed him to health – for she, too, had marvelled at his works, and grown a hunger of her own for the crafter of them, as different from the hunger of her father as she was from him.

In time, Weyland regained his strength, stout-hearted and dauntless, and Nithad came to him once more with his demand.

Once more, Weyland rcfuscd. Demanded freedom. Demanded his right to walk away.

King Nithad had two sons as well as a daughter, and where Nithad's hunger was for himself, and his cruelty born of appetite and thwarted wants, his sons enjoyed inflicting pain simply for the sake of it, and loved to watch things hurt and burn.

It was they who came to Weyland then, these sons, in his new cell atop the tallest, darkest tower of Nithad's darkened hall, and when his precious arms and hands were softly bound, safe and secure, his legs were tightly chained, and blocks of wood were put between to hold them hard, immovable.

As the elder brother held him there, the other took up Wadasearu, that great hammer, and with it broke the bones in Weyland's leg. He crushed the ankle sideways, that it could never heal. He shattered thigh and shin, and bound them so that they could never straighten again, and always would be weak.

The one who held him tight throughout, breathing in his pain, leant close and whispered to his ear, 'Now you will never walk away again.'

Then Weyland was a broken man.

Beadohild nursed him, as before, but he was changed now, and had wounds that could not heal. The more that Weyland retreated from himself, the more that Beadohild gave him of herself. Without understanding exactly when, she found she was in love with the broken, blazing talent of a man her father had imprisoned, and she found that she hated her brothers more than she thought it possible to hate.

Huddled in the pain of his disabling, though Weyland's mess of a body remained chained to Middle Earth, his mind and his heart escaped to the castle of his grandparents, and he walked then, painless and free through the land of Dream.

Weyland saw and did many strange things in Dream, as he waited for his body to heal, far below. He often found that he was in his cell, high atop the darkened tower of Nithad's hall. He found that he was weightless, then, and floated to the window, looked out at endless, stretching sky, and caught the legs of a passing eagle, which carried him weightless away with ease, to freedom, to find Wingelock in that sea of sky, and sail with his father to the hall of his grandparents, and on, to his great-grandfather, feasting at Woden's table.

Beadohild gave her days to tending him, and at night she slept there, holding him, hoping for the day when he would rouse.

When his weakened leg was as healed as ever it would be, and the wounds from his torture had settled to scars, and the cogs of Weyland's mind had cleared and his chest was free, Weyland woke to the land of waking, and Weyland returned to his broken body in the Middle Earth.

Beadohild kissed him when he did.

They held each other, then, and she kissed away his tears, and they lay with each other that night, in a secret known only to them.

Nithad, next day, came to him once more with his demands.

Weyland gave in, and set to work for the king.

The Flight of Weyland

When Aegil woke he felt a hunger in him as he never had before, so rich and hefty was the dwarven brew. He went out hunting then, and once he'd cleared his head took down some birds, to fill the table for Weyland and himself. When he returned, Weyland was nowhere to be seen.

And Weyland was nowhere to be seen that night, nor the next day, nor the day after that.

And Aegil spent his waking hours in search of his brother, and he spent his sleeping hours in Dream, calling his name. He would see him then, far, far above, clinging to the legs of an eagle, which carried him far, far away. Every night in Dream would Aegil chase him, calling and calling, to no avail.

And time passed, as time does, and Aegil grew sore worried for his brother, and sore afraid of what had befallen him.

One day, whilst out hunting birds to fill his belly, Aegil found himself craving some eggs to break his fast. He watched the birds, then, to find their nests, and remembered the old scavenging lesson of his childhood – to find the nest not from where the birds are going, but back from where they've been, for archers are not found at the place their arrows fall.

That night in Dream Aegil searched as usual, until he saw, high above, Weyland – clinging to his eagle as always he did. Instead of chasing, then, Aegil searched the sky to plot his route, and traced an idea of where the bird was flying from. Aegil backtracked, back from where they'd been.

Aegil saw, then, in the distance a great, dark hall, with a great, dark tower. Atop that tower, Aegil saw Weyland once more, waiting for him. And Weyland, in a dream of his own, looked down and saw his brother too. Both called; neither heard.

Aegil woke and set to searching, and asked of every passer-by in every shire, every homestead, every alehouse – asked for any who knew of a great, dark hall, with a great, dark tower. Finally, by a forgotten road he met an old and hooded man, who grimly leant upon a stick and told him, with what seemed malicious eye, where he might find that which he sought, and pointed him the way.

Aegil learned of Nithad, then, and Aegil learned of his hunger, and Aegil learned he was to blame.

And Aegil to the dark tower came.

Weyland was shut up in his cell, then, high atop Nithad's tower, eyes closed, trying to ignore the ever-constant pain of his leg, and the blistered ache of his never-resting hands, in hopes that he might visit Dream. With a faint but firm 'thunk', an arrow sank into the wall opposite his window. About it was tied a note.

Weyland checked the pain in his leg, confirmed that he was still awake, then heaved him up and hobbled over to unwrap the thing and read the single word: 'Brother.'

Weyland lurched to the window. There, far away, was Aegil. The men watched each other, silent from afar.

When Beadohild stole up to Weyland's cell he embraced her, with a life and passion to him that she had not seen since the houghing of his leg. Once they'd made love, and she lay in his arms, he described his brother to her, and told her she must seek him out in secret, somewhere along the bounds of her father's land. That when she found him she must tell him to gather the feathers of three hundred and thirty one birds, and when he had she must bring them all to Weyland's prison-forge.

And so she did.

And Weyland crafted then a strange, peculiar cloak of feathers. Thick it was, with crafty fastenings at the shoulder.

And Weyland asked his Beadohild, then, of her brothers. Of whether still her hate for them burned hot. She said it did. He told her to send them to him in his forge, the very next day, and to find some errand for the guards to go on when she did so.

This she did, and when the brothers entered, Weyland knocked them cold with Wadasearu.

When the eldest brother awoke, it was to the sound of Weyland working at his forge.

He tried to scream but found the pain too great. All about him was pain. He tried to move, and as he shuffled Weyland noticed he was awake, with a smile. Weyland put the tongs he was holding down, next to Wadasearu. Hobbled over and crouched close to his prisoner.

The brother tried to call the guards, but found that he no longer had a tongue. He tried to raise his hands to his face, but found instead a pair of stumps. He tried to get away from the smith, whose face was like fire in the light of the forge, but found no feet to obey his command. No legs, either. He started to wail.

'Do you seek your brother?' Weyland asked.

Weyland raised the tongs he had put down. Between the arms of the tool was a gilded skull. Weyland's prisoner wept, then, and Weyland leant in to his untouched ear and whispered, 'You will never walk away again.' He picked up Wadasearu, and beat his vanquished enemy's belly with it until the howling stopped.

From their eyes, Weyland crafted jewels. From their teeth he crafted brooches. Their spines became necklaces.

From their skulls he made a pair of goblets. Their arms made handles for blades, their legs made walking sticks.

Weyland made many other treasures from the bones and pieces of the sons of Nithad, that day. When he had finished, he told Beadohild to fetch him Mimming, along with the helmet and mail shirt that matched it, and the best wine from her father's stores. He asked her then to arrange for him to bestow his gifts upon Nithad and her mother in the hall, the following day.

This she did, and when she had she returned to him, Weyland hid his perfect battle-crafts within his dungeon-smithy, in a special hollow he had wrought for just such a purpose, which could not be found by any but the one he intended it for. This done, he filled the brother-goblets with the wine, and he and Beadohild laughed and drank. He added then a special ingredient, the ways of which were known only to Weyland, and together there they drank, and grew wild in embrace, and Weyland taught her how to visit Dream, and how to call Watling Street back from that Milky Way, and how to travel then beyond the world, beyond life, beyond time.

They made love once more, in the heat of his forge, in the blood of her brothers.

The next day Weyland took up Wadasearu and his tongs. He strapped on his feather cloak, gathered his brother-treasures into a bag, and kept the finest walking stick for himself. Thus set, he hobbled, slow, to that great, dark hall of Nithad, and there he found the thanes and earls of the court, and on his throne sat Nithad, and beside him sat his queen.

In front of all, then, Weyland bestowed upon the king the remains of his sons. The queen draped herself in her babies' finery, and Nithad drank from the skulls of his heirs. His best men were called forward, and each given blades crafted with princely parts.

When all was done, Weyland asked if he was pleased with his treasures. 'Most pleased,' replied the king. Weyland asked if the queen was pleased with her jewels. 'Most pleased,' replied the queen. Weyland asked if the king's men were pleased with their weapons. 'Most pleased,' replied the men in turn.

Weyland asked Nithad for his freedom, then. Asked to walk away.

Nithad simply laughed. 'Why should I let such a prize as you escape me? You will never walk away from here.'

Weyland smiled, and agreed.

In a strange, calm voice, Weyland told the king and told the queen and told the warriors how he had made each piece that now they wore and held, in merciless, abhorrent detail.

All was silent. The royal pair grew pale. He then described the baby boy that Beadohild held within the forge of her womb, and thanked the king for providing such a mother for his son.

Silence.

The king was braying, then, bellowing inhuman for his men to attack. Weyland jerked his back and the feathered cloak billowed up, split apart into a pair of wings, and Weyland flew about the hall, then, laughing, and out the window, and on, and far from the screaming of the king, and far from his dungeon-forge, and on he flew, back to Britain, back to his home.

And he never walked away again.

A Dance to the Music of Mimming

Weyland flew far from that dark tower, back to Britain, and never did return.

Nithad was an emptied man, thereafter, and grew to despise his daughter, and knew the only heir that he had left was also that of Weyland.

Beadohild lamented her lost love, and feared for her unborn child, and despised the court that she remained in – but in Dream she would visit Weyland still, and in Dream she would call his name, and in Dream they would meet again.

She had their son, and named him Wudga.

And deep within the hidden parts of Nithad's hall, deep within the dungeon-forge, Mimming sat beside the mail and helm who were his kin, and waited.

For thirteen years Mimming sang for his master.

Wudga was twelve years old when he answered the call, and deep within the long unentered forge, he there took up that mail and wore it, and there took up that helm and placed it on his head, and there he held that Mimming in his hand. There he became a man.

And Wudga then turned wreccan. Left without saying goodbye.

With his heir gone, then, old, cruel Nithad demanded the death of his daughter. As Beadohild was marched to the hall, she stood brave and resolute, surrounded by uneasy thanes, waiting for the death-blow to fall.

With a faint but firm 'thunk', an arrow sank into the throat of the man holding her, and he in turn sank to his knees. With further thunks, the men surrounding her were similarly felled. Beadohild ran, then, through the doorway where Aegil drew back his bow. The pair fled through turns and twists of Nithad's hall, finding exit after exit blocked, until the only route left to them led up.

Barricaded in Weyland's dusty tower-cell, Aegil looked out of the window to see the pyre that was being constructed at the base of the dark tower. He shot at the men below who built it, killing many, but in time ran out of arrows.

As Aegil stared out at the fires being lit below, he noticed Nithad barking instructions. Aegil turned and saw the arrow still sunk into the wall, the arrow that he'd shot thirteen years before, and he shot it once again through Nithad's throat.

The flames bit higher, and higher. The smoke grew thick.

As the tower began to heave and strain, readying its collapse, Aegil took Beadohild's hand, wrenched, and threw her out the window. With a brief glance back to the burning cell, he looked the grim, old, hooded man who stood in the doorway right in the eye, and jumped.

Aegil picked himself up from the deck of Wingelock and, laughing, embraced his father, before introducing the bemused Beadohild.

They sailed back, then, to Britain, to Weyland.

But Wudga roamed the land thereafter, with Mimming as his guide. He came, in time, to seek Theodric, that famous fighter. Asked after him in every ale house and every hall, until finally three men blocked his path, and asked him why he asked his questions.

'I seek to know adventure. Theodric's the man to teach me.'

'I am Hildebrand, and serve Theodric. We have no need of dwarves. Get you away.'

'I am Wudga, son of Weyland, son of Wade, son of Wada, born of Waellende Wulf. I am no dwarf, and if you doubt my battle craft, then put me to the test.'

And so a duel was there agreed, to take the proper measure of this Wudga. First fought he with Hama, who did enjoy the fight and find himself well matched, and as they danced the dance of combat there they found themselves fine partners, and built a bond between them everlasting.

Soon Hama did step out, impressed, and Hildebrand took up the fight. And Mimming sang, and guided Wudga's hand through air, and weaved and bobbed and jerked and did with ease defend and foin, deflect and counter-cut all that wise Hildebrand could offer. Hildebrand was impressed, and gazed there at that Mimming.

Their third then took his place, and he was not impressed. He had no interest in jumped-up boys. The fight between them played with an intensity and edge hitherto unknown, and when Mimming finally had knocked him to the ground and held him by the throat and he had called for quarter, as Wudga, smiling, withdrew his blade and turned to face the others, to see if he had passed the test, that craven third whose name shan't be recorded, in his humiliated rage, removed a long knife from a hidden place, and lunged.

Mimming, though, is ever alert.

Before Wudga knew it his arm was extended, and his blade plunged through the man's neck.

So Wudga joined them then, and took the corpse's place.

As the three wended their way towards Theodric, they had adventures and had battles, and Wudga and Hama found themselves firm companions, and Hildebrand saw first-hand the power of that Mimming – a power too great to be entrusted to an unknown youth. He had, in secret, a replica made, and once this forgery was forged he swapped the swords as Wudga slept, and kept that shining Mimming hidden, for himself.

So Wudga was brought to Theodric, that mighty battle-leader, and Theodric was told of the death of the man that Wudga had replaced.

'I cannot have a man whose worth I do not know fight in my name.'

And Theodric challenged him then to a duel, and Wudga once more accepted, and Theodric was on him, raging. As they fought, the armour was cleaved from Theodric, so hard did Wudga fight to defend himself, but the helm and mail of Weyland held ever true. Finally, the false Mimming split under Theodric's merciless blows, and he had Wudga by the throat, as Wudga had the man that he'd replaced.

Wudga smiled, and he conceded.

Theodric did not smile. Theodric raised his blade to remove the head of Wudga from his shoulders.

Hama then heard something call to him. Heard something screaming in song. From Hildebrand's battle-bag he heard the howl of Mimming, and in a flash he understood, and leapt then to unsheathe the wondrous blade, and as he did its song did echo out and all were shaken, and he threw the sword to Wudga then, who caught it just in time, and Theodric's blade did shatter when it met that mighty jewel of Weyland.

And Wudga was displeased.

And full in battle-dress, then, his helm and shirt still strong, his roaring birthright demanding satisfaction, he leapt at Theodric, who had by now but rags and shards and tatters of what once he'd worn. Hildebrand threw him another weapon, but that too was cleaved by the blows of Mimming. Another sword did Hildebrand throw then, that too decimated. Finally, as outraged Wudga was ready to land the killing stroke, Hama leapt forth and stood between them. Mimming pulled back, just in time.

'For my sake, Wudga, spare his life.'

And Wudga resheathed Mimming, and extended a hand, and helped Theodric to his feet.

When all were calmer, Theodric was overjoyed at the prowess of this new stranger to his court, and did apologise for anger, and bid him pledge allegiance and join him as shoulder-companion, one of his mighty three, and gave him rings and gold and honour.

Once Wudga swore on oath to serve Theodric well, Hildebrand advised that Mimming was too powerful for any but Theodric to wield. Theodric, remembering well the duel he had lost, agreed. As Wudga slept, Mimming was taken from him once more. When he woke he was told that, as part of his pledge, the blade must be given up, replaced with a sword of Theodric's choosing.

Wudga was not pleased, and Hama was dismayed at the slyness. Mimming raged at his kidnap, and sang to them of the insult from afar.

Wudga and Hama fought many fights, and wandered many lands together. Whilst Wudga's helm and mail stayed strong and true, no sword could satisfy him. When, in time, a messenger from Hildebrand arrived, calling once again for aid, faint on the wind the distant song of Mimming met their ears.

Theodric was held captive, it seemed, by ettins. To win his freedom a great tournament of heroes would be held, and many duels raged, then, and even Theodric was given leave to fight.

It came down, finally, after much blood shed on either side, to a fight of honour between Wudga and the ettin-king, who fought well, and towered over the Wade-ling. Each blow landed knocked him hard, but the crafty mail shirt absorbed the blows, and the wise helmet kept his skull quite safe. The bludgeonings of the giant, though, rent Wudga's sword in two with ease, and Wudga leapt and landed on the giant's back, and gripped about his throat, and clawed his eyes, but had no weapon for to close the kill.

Mimming screamed in song.

Screamed to Theodric to send him to his master, but even then, with all their lives in peril, Theodric was loath to lose the blade, and Hama pleaded with him, and Hildebrand as well, and Wudga, clinging on for life and gripping hard the bucking foe, called out for Mimming.

Theodric gave in, and hurled the blade, which flew through air into the hand of Wudga, who plunged it in the eyes of the ettin, through into his brain, and sliced the top of his head clean off, then rode the corpse as it fell to ground.

Much feasting then was had, once that heroic band had travelled on to safer hall, and deep in cups they were when, overjoyed, Theodric gave praise to Wudga, thanks, and promised him reward: 'Anything you please, half of all that's mine to give.'

Wudga replied that he would not be greedy, requesting three things only. Freedom for himself, freedom for Hama, and freedom for Mimming.

Theodric's joy sank instantly. But he was bound, and had been witnessed, and at that moment word came to the hall of strife in Theodric's home, and he and his men departed at once.

And Wudga and Hama and Mimming were free.

They roamed then, and had many fine and free adventures together.

One tale tells of the beauty of a girl named Maethilde, and of the combat-brothers' contest to woo her. Hama performed such feats, and tried his all, receiving nothing but a sigh. Wudga did the same, and the shining beauty simply rolled her eyes.

But Wudga knew that only when you've given up can you be said to fail. On he pestered the girl, declaring that as she was a radiant Maethilde, so he would royal Geat be, and sing at her window and whelm her with his love. Every night she woke to Wudga singing songs of Geat and Maethilde, until she grew quite mad with lack of sleep, and wearied of his games, and seemed to shift her stance. Her manner, then, was soft and kind to Wudga, and she framed her face most wonderfully, and stoked his fires until they were unbearable, and Mimming stiffened in his sheath and urged him ever on.

As the two shared cups one eve, she leant in close, stroked finger up his thigh, and whispered of what she would do, that night within her bed.

Wudga was enslaved.

Maethilde commanded he must come to her tomorrow night, and would be satisfied.

Wudga lay abed, then, sleepless at the thoughts of what would follow.

Weary the next day, but powered by a raging fire within, he sought Maethilde, who somehow was more beautiful than ever she had been before, and as she laid a hand on him she whispered that she had a headache, and promised that tomorrow night would be their night. Wudga was lost, and Mimming ached in his sheath as she left them.

That night, Wudga lay in bed once more, sleepless still at thoughts of what would follow.

So Wudga was a wearied man indeed, next day, but desperate still for that Maethilde, who cooed and stroked him yet again, and whispered that tonight would be their night, and told him then at midnight for to come and join her in her rooms, and told him where to find her in the darkness.

And Wudga waited, Mimming's ache unbearable, and on he went to wait as he had been instructed in the muddied ditch outside her house.

He waited there, in wet and cold, three hours until the lights were all extinguished from the house. Weary-tired, and stinking cold, he clambered up and crept towards the door. Wudga opened it.

Inside were lines of men with swords, and Wudga turned and fled and hid himself, leapt back into the darkling ditch. Waited for the men to pass, another hour, and then two more, and three more after that. Stinking, scratched and now exhausted, but with fire hotter than ever and Mimming burning in his sheath, Wudga crept again, past the sleeping soldiers, until he found the door he knew would bring him to his joy.

In darkness he eased it open, eased himself into bed and felt the hot wetness of a hungry mouth against his own.

And then he smelled her breath.

Wudga pushed the dog away. A yapping bitch on heat was all the bed there held. Mimming howled, and Wudga felt full woe. He crept, back past snoring soldiers, back through mud in dark, and crashed alone in bed for three days and three nights, with Mimming tossed wherever he would land, unsatisfied.

When Hama had finished laughing at the tale, and Mimming had been oiled and sharpened once more, the two men drank to that Maethilde, as cunning as she was beautiful, and wished her only well.

In time, Theodric was displaced by his cruel uncle, that Eormanric of wolven mind; sent into an exile lasting thirty years, in great King Aetla's court, and ruled the city of the Maerings as his under-king. Eormanric with much wealth bought the service of our pair, and so Wudga and Hama pledged allegiance to him, and no attempts were made to take that noble Mimming from its master.

Often, in that time, hissing in flight yelled the spear from our battle-brothers, at peoples fierce. They fought against their former master, also, and many fragments of the Ealdspell call them traitors, and many others heroes. Wudga and Hama grew old in battle, then, and came to see their hunt for the adventure that would fill them as fruitless as the hunt for Maethilde's love.

When Eormanric died, Wudga found himself out of love with death, and disdainful of his many deeds. He took that great blade Mimming, then, and bid the world farewell, and travelled to an ancient rock in which he slid the blade up past its pommel, as easily as knife in butter. Mimming wept in stone, there, and Wudga wept without.

Wudga and Hama travelled then without a master once more, and never did seek battle again. They made their way to Britain, and lived a fine retirement with Beadohild and Weyland, and their barrow-graves can still be found there to this day.

But Weyland did not die, and lived to see them all decease.

Weary, then, alone in his barrow-forge, the elves did there unlock the door to Elfland, and there he was apprenticed to that radiant sun, the spirit of flame, the greatest of the elvish smiths, and mastered and was all craft, undying, transcendent.

And Mimming stayed in blackness for what could have been an instant and could have been an age, and sang unheard his mournful lament, deep within the rock, and gave up hope, alone in stone.

Until the sound of hammer disturbed his song.

And a chunk of stone dislodged, and there his hilt was fresh exposed, and Waldere gripped the sword of Weyland, and pulled that Mimming from the stone, and loud he sang his battle-song anew, and on then went that Waldere, on to Aetla's lands, to start a new adventure of his own, which I shall not tell here, though many others have and will.

They say the song of Mimming sings loud still, for those few that can hear it, and Weyland works still in his smithy, still crafting Mimming's kin, elf-wise now and endless – hungry to teach his skills and immortality. Many since have sought apprenticeship, though none have yet proved worthy.

Perhaps you'll be the first.

The Wife's Lament

The fire of torches could be seen, then, through the windows of the richly laden hall. Though it was deep in night, red light shone, and their hosts could be heard outside the thick, wooden door. Inside, Hnaef smiled a sad smile, the gold of the flame without flickering 'cross his face. He stood, drew that famous blade, Hildeleoma, and spoke to his men.

'This is not the dawn, nor a dragon flying past, nor are the gables of this hall aflame. Nay. It is men who approach, battle-ready. Raven and eagle cry, wolf howls, spears clash and shield answers shaft. Now the moon has hidden behind the clouds, woeful deeds begin that will bring to a bitter end this enmity. Awaken now, my warriors!'

And so they did. As attack came the sixty men fought valiant. Their hosts broke bonds of hospitality, broke bonds of kinship, and father killed son that day. Hnaef too felt blade bite deep, though his courage was unmatched by any. A good lord.

Many, many years before, a boat had drifted onto shore, and on that boat was not a single crewman, not a single passenger save for a single baby boy. That baby boy was lain upon a shield, and surrounding him were ancient and forgotten blades, and there amongst them was that ettin-blade, great Hildeleoma. The baby boy who lay there had a faded scar across him, older far than he could possibly have been.

And the people upon whose shore this boy had landed took the arrival of this boat as a sign, for their king had been a cruel and grasping man, whose name was Heremod (and who you may recall). When he had fled they found themselves at war, and with the weapons from the ship they fought and won, and the baby boy they named their Scyld, and as they did a look of recognition crossed the age-old infant's eyes, and he was raised to be their king, and a fine and honoured king he was, all that his predecessor wasn't.

When Scyld died, many-wintered, he returned once more to the waves, back in that great ship, as first he had come. His line took his name, and ruled thereafter, and were known as the Scyldings.

Through the sea of time this royal clan sailed, and many rulers and great warriors and wise ones were born from it. To the Anglo-Saxons and their cousin tribes, kingship was not a birthright to the individual, but rather to the bloodline – on the death of every king the witan, or

wise council, would meet to elect a new king from the Scylding line, which sometimes was the old king's son, sometimes brother, sometimes other kin. But all descended from Scyld, and all thus were Scyldings, as had Hnaef been.

We have told, thus far, many tales of mighty men from the Ealdspell. It is true that in the dark and glorious days of the heroic age, when life was cheap, and strength and fight was all, it was the deeds of men that most held notice. But women were no underlings.

In fact, when men were made and slaved in war and forced to hold to hardy ways and die for others, women were all the more important. It was women who rose above such things. It was women who salved the unquenched flames of hatred and of honour, who dulled the blade of battle into one of peace, and brought their people to a better, wiser place.

They called these women peaceweavers. Hildeburh was such a woman.

Hnaef had been her brother. She had married the king of their Frisian enemy, Finn, to weave a peace between their peoples. It had worked, for a time. She bore that Finn a son, named (some say) Frithuwulf, and he was fostered to his uncle in Hnaef's hall, Hildeburh's homeland. Such noble fostering was common practice, then, from seven or eight to fourteen or fifteen. In this way were bonds of loyalty forged, and of peace, and when the child came of age he'd join his foster father's dryht, and fight for him, a man.

When Frithuwulf had come of age, Hnaef and his men were invited by Finn as honoured guests, to enjoy his hall and hospitality through the harsh Yuletide season. Honourable men, all, they heartily accepted, and came as they were bid.

Nobody agrees how first the fight began – some say a tribal feud between Jutes on either side, some say that ettins and strange magics were involved. Some say other things, but it little matters. The result was the same. The bonds of hospitality were broken, and Hnaef and his men were betrayed. They barricaded themselves in Finn's hall to fight off the battle-hungry soldiers that surrounded them, and this is how we began our tale.

Five days the siege went on, and though no death was dealt to Hnaef's men in the hall, sore much was dealt to Finn's outside. Finally a desperate, last assault did come, which cost that noble Hnaef his life, and Frithuwulf as well. But still defenders did defend, and Finn was there repelled. No choice was left for either side but truce 'twixt Finn and Hunlafing (who was in charge now Hnaef was dead).

So Hildeburh lost her brother and her son there, as her weak husband bowed to forces of hate and of herd. She felt the peace unweave, and could not stop it doing so. All this and more roiled in her chest as the heat of a funeral fire warmed her face.

On the pyre before her were bloodstained, broken shirts of mail, finely wrought and dented crests of helm and brooch. Into flame went Hildeleoma, Hnaef's great, gilded ettin-sword. Hildeburh bade the men to add her son to the blaze, to burn him body and bone, to lay him by his uncle's side. This they did. The reek of it mounted high, thick in clouds, and Hildeburh forced herself to bear it. Heads collapsed, wounds burst, blood sprang away from the cruel bite of flame. That greediest of things devoured the flesh of those whom war had carried off. Men of both sides burned together in death, their glory now departed.

According to the agreement struck, all hostility was to cease. Hnaef's men temporarily to become Finn's, be given food and board and payment until the rough seas had passed and they were able to return to their land. It was supposed to be just a few months.

But Geofon is a fickle mistress.

Well over a year did they remain, and for a second Yuletide, and sore did they disdain their hosts, and nod in cold lament on the anniversary of their betrayal, and drink to Hnaef and Frithuwulf, and much did they desire their homeland.

One in particular, a wreccan Jute named Hengest, who men called the Stallion, felt mod burn in his chest, and hate grow in his heart. When, one day, a son of Hunlaf laid in his lap that famous Hildeleoma, the blade that all had seen destroyed in flame, Hengest gripped it burning in his hand, and accepted it.

There was a code of honour in the Anglo-Saxon tribes that we call by its Latin name, the *comitatus*, and which in English tongue is called the dryht. By this code a warrior prized courage and loyalty above all things, and certainly above his life. A glorious death, blessed by Hretha, would give a life of fame amongst men, and earn a place in Woden's hall – the men of the comitatus were modig indeed. To survive their leader, however, and retreat from the battlefield, meant lifelong disgrace and infamy. Shame which could not be dispelled.

Whilst the lord they'd sworn fealty to was yet alive, the warrior owed him loyalty unto death – should that lord be slain, the man was honour-bound to avenge him. Or die trying. The lord was bound, also, to be generous with his men, and to hold a courage even beyond their own – there was no greater shame for such a leader than to be outdone in bravery by one of his followers. The leader's life was given to victory; the followers' to their leader.

It is this comitatus, this dryht, which helps explain the true horror of that Heremod, the battle-heat of Suanus, or the betrayal of Wudga. It is this dryht that helps explain the deep and gnawing shame of Hengest, who sat through yet another Yule, whilst the ashes of his lord lay unavenged, and the men who made them were laughing at their feast, and Hengest did survive.

It helps explain why, when Hnaef's still-living Danish men did board their ships and finally depart, Hengest would not leave, would not retreat the site of death, and stayed instead as follower of Finn. It helps explain why Hnaef's men did return, with many, many more.

It helps explain why Hildburh and Hengest let them all into the hall of Finn, and led them then in wholesale slaughter, and why Finn and his men were killed that day in brutal vengeance for the murdered Hnaef and Frithuwulf; to slake the honour of the Scyldings.

So Hildeburh lost her husband, then, as she had her brother and her son, but felt a peace rewoven from the threads. All this and more roiled in her chest as the wind cooled her face, stood on the bow of the gold-laden victory-ship, returned once more to the waves, and left the reddened hall behind. Heading home as first she had come.

Back to the Scyldings.

The
Stallion
and the
Horse

Hengest turned wreccan once more, and as the Scyldings returned to their home, so Hengest continued his noble exile. With his brother, Horsa, Hengest saw many lands, and offered many kings the use of his sword, and much battle was waged, and much honour won across the Middle Earth.

It was in AD 449 that Hengest and Horsa came finally to Britain, at a place we now call Ebbsfleet, in what would become the Kingdom of Kent.

This land they walked was a shining land, green and pleasant. A land that felt more like a home to them than any from which they'd come. This part of Britain then was the domain of Wurtgern.

Hengest and Horsa had not come to his realm by chance.

For Wurtgern was a wicked king, who let his darkest parts have reign. Much hate he held for other British tribes, and warred with them unendingly, and his most brutal hate was for the Picts, who dwelt in what today is Scotland.

When battle turned and Hretha favoured them at last, the Picts pushed on, taking war to Wurtgern's borders, slaughtering hard the Britons that had tried to slaughter them.

And Wurtgern was afeared.

First he called to Rome for aid, but they were busy warring with King Aetla, Theodric, Waldere and the rest, far to the east. They could not, would not, offer help.

But word had come to Wurtgern of three ships that coursed the waters, led by noble brothers, wreccan then and wandering, who had a hardy troop of loyal, mighty men with them, and who in search of their adventures and a home to earn, would offer might to any king who asked it of them. Wurtgern sent his ships to call upon the swords of Hengest and of Horsa, to offer, in exchange for battle, land for them to settle.

This they did, for Hengest now did long to feel a steady bed beneath his head, to root into the earth, and give himself once more unto a homeland.

So Hengest and Horsa came to Britain, then, and to earn their home anew they battled Wurtgern's foes, and risked their lives in service. Hengest's men were strong and wild, and the Pictish troops, though fierce, had grown too used to fighting weak and heartless forces, and so were not a match for the comitatus that they met.

Wurtgern was overjoyed, and gave the troops of Hengest and of Horsa much land in Kent to call their own, and Hengest sent word back to all the kings that he had fought for, word of the weakness of Wurtgern's fighting men, of the need he had for strong troops, of the bountiful, beautiful land of Britain.

So it was that wave on wave of tribes did come, as word did spread; Angles and Saxons, Frisians and Jutes, and many more besides. Amongst them were Hengest's family, a strong and noble son named Aesc, and a beautiful daughter called by some Rowena.

Scyldings came, too, and to them was granted Kentish land all of their own, including what today is Harty Island, in honour of great Hnaef, for Hengest still felt shame at that lost king.

Wurtgern welcomed all. Each wave he added to his army, sent them on further, bloody raids to beat into submission all the British tribes who weren't his own. As all these many Anglo-Saxon peoples arrived, and found a world of bounty and of wealth, they worked hard for Wurtgern, faced many terrors, battled many foes, lost many good men in earning the land they loved.

Years passed and, soon enough, Wurtgern would let no man of his own tribe risk life or limb; instead he risked the lives of Anglo-Saxons. As they took all the risk, so Wurtgern took reward, and Wurtgern was triumphal. The Picts stayed cowed up far away. The Irish did not dare to interfere. Wurtgern's Britons grew fat and cruel and complacent, with their Anglo-Saxon battle-servants doing all their fighting for them.

Soon enough, in fact, Wurtgern failed to see why he still needed them around.

His enemies were weakened now, and kept far from his borders. Why should he continue to allow these blade-mongers presence in his kingdom? At the very least they should be paying for the privilege. And did they need so very much land? So many farms? So many children? Send them home, back to where they came from, their use was served now.

Their numbers had, it's true, grown large indeed, and they had earned with blood extensive land across the east. Other English dwelt in Britain too – the Jutes of the Wihtwara Isle and the Ytene Forest, the people of that Sigemund in the north, and Offa to the west.

Wurtgern had them all informed their time was up. That most of them would have to leave, their lands and homesteads forfeit. A small contingent of hand-selected warriors would be allowed to remain, for now, so long as they stayed servile to him.

The Anglo-Saxons did not receive the insult well.

Hengest did his best to calm the rage and hurt that echoed through the land, and assured them all that something must be wrong, that somewhere things were misconstrued. They had been loyal to Wurtgern as no others had, and had fought hard for him, and won him all he now enjoyed – even he could not betray such an oath.

Hengest invited the king and his men to a feast in his hall on Thanet, to reach an accord and understand the discontent. No sword or shield or weaponry would be allowed, on either side, for peace and amity were the only aims. Wurtgern arrived with his nobles, dressed in finery, with soft skin and soft hands and scornful looks upon their brows. They laughed at the food, they laughed at the brutishness of the men, they laughed at the songs which were sung. They did not laugh at the drink, and called again and again for mead and for ale. Again, and again.

In not too long, Wurtgern and his men were drunk.

Hengest found an anger growing in his breast. Still, he wore the mask and smiled, for his men were insulted – if Hengest let his fire rise then so would they. He had to set an example.

Wurtgern drank and drank, cackling louder as he did so. Three times Hengest tried to raise the issue of land, three times he was rebuffed.

It was the custom then, for the noblest women of the hall to serve the noblest guests their mead, as a gesture of respect. So it was that, as a sign of honour, Rowena served Wurtgern and his aristocrats. Again and again they called her back, to fill their horns, to fill their gullets. With every fresh trip they leered harder, groped at her further.

Finally Wurtgern grabbed her waist and pulled her onto him, cheered on by his drunk, soft-handed men – pressed her into his lap and tore her gown, pawing, forcing his stinking, reddened, drunken face against hers, pulling at her hair to keep her in place.

The music stopped.

The Anglo-Saxons stopped.

Hengest stopped.

All stared at Wurtgern. Wurtgern didn't seem to notice. Rowena slapped him in the face and pulled away, as Wurtgern and his courtiers laughed oblivious, safe in the weaponless hall. 'Fine meat you provide, for a foreigner,' the drunken king called to Hengest. 'Give me your daughter and maybe you can keep your land!'

The soft-hands crowed. Wurtgern grabbed Rowena once more.

Hengest felt his chest-fire seethe.

As he glowed white-hot and battle-shone, Hengest stood full tall, towering then above the room, and roared to all the Anglo-Saxons there, 'Use your knives!'

In a heartbeat each and every one had taken from their plate the angled knives they'd eaten with, and felt the rage which had been brewing rise, and grabbed the nearest of Wurtgern's men and let the metal feed on blood.

The only Briton allowed to leave that night was Wurtgern, stripped and bloodied, and that out of respect for rank, and oath, and honour. Hengest told him to meet in battle thirteen days hence, at Aylesford.

Still drunk and babbling, the terrified Wurtgern fled, soiling himself, and left his men to the mercy of the Anglo-Saxon blade.

It did not have much.

The day of battle came. Wurtgern held all the forces he could muster, endless men from all across his kingdom, hard conscripted in, alongside what soldiers and bodyguards he had left, and all the mercenaries he could find at such short notice, hoping that by sheer force of numbers he might overwhelm Hengest in his rage.

He almost did.

For though the Anglo-Saxons were many, their numbers still could not compare to those of Wurtgern's men, and they fought and fought, and killed and killed, but on and on came wave on wave of Wurtgern's sacrificial lambs (for he cared not how many lives he threw away), and finally Horsa was slain. Thus Hengest's brother died, and great woe echoed then through the ranks of the Anglo-Saxons, and Wurtgern cackled that he would pierce Rowena too, when day was done.

Then Hengest's allies came.

For Hengest had, as soon as Wurtgern fled from the feast, sent messengers up to the Picts, out to the Irish, far to the Scyldings, down to the southern Jutes, along to northern kin and westerfolk, and on to all the little nations of the peoples who cruel Wurtgern ruled. Asked all of them to join him now, and fight against the tyrant.

And every one did come that day.

The battle was immense, and Wurtgern's army decimated. His Britons fled to the hills, where hordes of Picts pursued and butchered them.

Victory was Hengest's, and he had Horsa buried then beneath a great monument, on which was carven a great, white horse, which stood for many centuries, and paid great honour to him. In the land of Kent they ruled, thereafter, and gave great thanks to all who'd come unto their aid, and made alliances afresh, and granted further territories for all, and shared the plunder from Wertgurn's hall amongst the many tribes who'd fought that day.

Wurtgern did not die then, but fled from battle, leaving his subjects to the blade once more. The Britons, after time, regrouped, electing a new king, descended from the Roman occupiers who were remembered still. Aurelius Ambrosius, they called him. The first thing he did was seek out Wurtgern, hidden in his high tower. He was discovered there, incestuous with his daughter; a child they bore between them.

When he could not gain entry, Ambrosius simply set the tower aflame. Wurtgern, his daughter, and his grandson-son were cooked alive by the people he'd abandoned.

For many years the battles boiled on – the Anglo-Saxon alliance of Picts and other peoples against the realm that had been Wurtgern's, and now belonged to Ambrosius. And this new leader was a fine leader.

With Horsa dead, Aesc was Hengest's second in command, and together they caused much slaughter, and fought well for peoples who had known only pain and cruelty under Wurtgern. Two years later, in AD 457 at the Battle of Crayford, Hengest and Aesc took Kent in its entirety, and won the kingdom for their own.

Hengest reigned as King of Kent, then, for another thirty-one winters, and led many battles, and won much, much good for his people before passing on to the hall of Woden to be with his brother once more – the stallion returning to the horse. He was buried at what today is Hengistbury Head, in Dorset – a permanent sentinel to ward off invasion.

Some say they see him there still, every-guarding his hard-won home.

Heorot
Returned

In Harty Isle did Hrothgar, king, a stately, gilded hall decree, which was surrounded then by fens, a mile then 'til the water ends, on other side the sea.

Of that line of Scyldings, the greatest in battle of the kings of their realm was Healfdean, and it was to him that Hengest had gifted land in Kent, in penance for the death of Hnaef.

Healfdean had four children, and each was a gifted child, who grew to gifted adulthood – a golden brood, and Scyldings through and through.

Eldest was Heorogar, the noblest, most modig man who had been born amongst his people in memory, who ever held true to causes of honour.

Youngest of the sons was Halga, the bravest ever known, always ready to rush to risk, to take what he desired, and damn the fear of all that followed. Younger still was an elf-bright sister. Some say her name was Yrsa, but most remain silent when asked of her, for a shame which cannot be spoken of directly. Hers was a pure mind and an innocent beauty, as perfect and brittle as starlight, and as loving as the sun.

The middle son was Hrothgar, and it was he who held the greatest gift of all.

Hrothgar was wise.

For many years a war-feud had raged between Healfdean's people and those known as Heathobards, or War-beards. It was in these raging battle-times that Frodo, King of the Heathobards, met Healfdean on the field, and Healfdean was mercilessly slain.

Heorogar, the eldest, was elected king in his stead, and was a noble king, and this noble king sought vengeance for his father, to slake the blood-feud that honour bound him to. This Scylding king held close to honour, and so he quickly died an honourable death – for honour alone is little strength against dishonourable foes. He too met the fate of his father before him, and Frodo it was who took his life in the field.

The kingship now sailed on to Hrothgar, and here it lingered. For as great a king as honour can create, wisdom is by far the finer forge. He held a witan, first, to choose how best to follow on from loss of Heorogar. Halga spoke the loudest, demanding blood for blood, bone for bone – offering to command a mighty rush against the enemy.

Hrothgar thought.

In open combat Halga led the charge, and the full force of Frodo's War-

beards met them, and spear clattered against wood. Hrothgar, as we have said, was wise, with wisdom enough to let Halga use his courage and his boldness as best he could. As Halga's horde raged and the Heathobards tired, from all about the field of battle, hidden in the woods, came other men – men who'd spent the fight thus far spreading round to cut the War-beards off from their retreat. Led by Hrothgar, this cunning force crashed down, enveloping Frodo and his men, and thus the war was won.

Frodo met his death at Hrothgar's hand that day.

Halga demanded more.

For the Scyldings had lost two kings to the foe – why should the War-beards not pay the same? Frodo first, and his son, Ingeld, second. The blood-feud demanded it, cried Halga; honour must be served. And Hrothgar was tempted, for he was wounded also at the loss of his kin, and diving to those deep waters was an attractive proposition indeed.

But Hrothgar, as we have said, was wise.

Hrothgar knew the endless depth of such a mere, and knew the danger. He vowed to end the feud, and so proclaimed that Frodo's death sufficed, and Ingeld would be spared. To secure this new alliance, Hrothgar's only daughter, Freawaru, would marry Frodo's heir as peaceweaver, to join Scyldings with Heathobards in amity and kinship.

So Frodo was succeeded by his son Ingeld, whose heart was not ruled by honour, whose mod lacked courage; who was not wise.

Now it came into Hrothgar's vast mind to command the construction of a mead hall, greater than Middle Earth had known, to conclude the bitterness of battle and loss, and to share glory with young and old alike. For this unprecedented hall, Hrothgar knew that more than Scylding-craft would be required, and so he searched his kingdom for the perfect site, and found it in that newest portion, there amongst the fens of Kent, on the island we today call Harty, gifted by Hengest in honour of Hnaef.

The hall would be named Heorot, and it would be unique – for Hrothgar did not build from scratch, but rather took the grand and entish ruins of a great and spreading Roman structure. This he commanded there to be restored, and grown anew, and to be spun without in shining gold, and for the floors of bright mosaic to be made rich once more. The hall towered high, with hornéd gables wide, and there was music of the harp, then, and the stories of scops.

For a time, the glories of Harty were magnificent. Though Hrothgar kept many halls across his kingdoms, his happiest times were spent in splendour at Heorot, and it was there, when he began to grow old, that Hrothgar did retire.

He was joined by his nephew, Hrothulf, who was not the son of Heorogar, and had reason to believe himself Hrothgar's heir. But such beliefs are dangerous things. Not long after Hrothulf's arrival in Kent, Hrothgar found himself a wife (for the mother of Freawaru had died long ago). Wealhtheow was her name, and she was strong and young, and came from the English tribe who then ruled in East Anglia – the Wuffingas. Hrothgar's wisdom did attract her greatly, and she bore him two plump, healthy sons, whose names were Hrethric and Hrothmund.

Time is treacherous, however, and fickle.

Heorot had been built on that island due in part to its natural defences, sitting as it did at the heart of the Schrawynghop, the marsh of monsters. This stretching wetland would have been no easy thing for any army to cross, even were it not for the terrors and the horrors that inhabited it.

It was this, of course, which proved Heorot's undoing.

Night after night, year after year, the laughter and the merriment of Heorot echoed about the Schrawynghop, and night after night, year after year, they reached the ears of a thing called Grendel, and they tormented him, and cut like knives. Grendel was young, then, and as he grew in length and strength he grew to hate the place that caused him such unending pain. When he was grown full strong enough, he went to make them stop.

When first Grendel walked through night to enter the hall, he found the company sleeping, and not a fear amongst them.

When morning came, thirty men were dead, the hall reddened.

The next night it happened again.

On and on was wrought the malice of Grendel, glutting and gorging on the corpses of his foe, and sad songs were sung about the Middle Earth, and for twelve long years Grendel held sway amongst the marshes of the Schrawynghop, and all who sought him were killed, for no blade could penetrate his hide, and the weapon could not be found to harm him. So it was, that greatest of halls lay empty, night after night, and the gods gave no assistance, and no counsel sufficed, and Hrothgar despaired, and Hrothgar wearied.

Though Ingeld owed all to Hrothgar's mercy and wisdom, when messengers came to beg for help none was forthcoming, for Ingeld held tight to his luxuries, and cared not for the man who had made them – cared only for the feast, and not a whit for the founder.

As the thirteenth year began, so came a visitor.

Folk whispered that his name was Beowulf, kin to that King Hygelac from across the sea. Hrothgar knew the name, and had known him as a child, and knew him now to be of heart most stout, and with the strength of many men in battle, though not overwise in weapon-craft.

So Beowulf was welcomed heartily to Heorot, and Hrothgar gave a mighty feast, and that night Beowulf and his men took to the hall, and each beneath the gilding slept soundly.

All but for Beowulf.

And so it was he heard, awake in darkling hour, the gliding round about the walls of Grendel, shadow-dweller, the walker in the night. He listened to the soft and searching steps that circled then the hall.

The door gave way at Grendel's touch, and silent he stalked across the bright mosaic floor, towards the sleeping men to make his meal. The first he groped at, tore great gobbets from him, sucked at veins and in no time had eaten down to fingers and to feet.

Grendel grabbed another man, excited now to feast.

That man was Beowulf.

And as the great and monstrous claw seized him, Beowulf in turn seized the claw, and gripped and twisted, and Grendel shrieked, and as they wrassled there unarmed, muscles prised apart, there came a snapping of tendons, bone-locks burst, and Beowulf tore the arm from out the shoulder, ripping flesh and gristle alike.

And Grendel screamed.

Fled the hall, fled to night, blood flowing, impossible to staunch.

So Grendel was defeated.

And there was feasting and rejoicing, and Hrothgar bestowed much honour and many gifts on Beowulf and his men, and all gave hearty praises then, and drank, and ate, and sang songs of the triumph of Beowulf. All fell that night to happy, fretless sleep – the first the hall had known in almost thirteen years – and high above the door was hung that monstrous arm, a token there of victory.

When Beowulf awoke, it was to death and slaughter.

Around him were the arms and legs and parts of men who had but hours before been laughing, joyful. Blood once more flowed through the hall, and in the doorway a creature greater still than Grendel reached to pluck the arm she knew so well from up above the door, catching yet another warrior who lunged to stop her, and carrying both away into the night.

Grief then came in waves, and Beowulf took up the blade called Hrunting, from he who sat at Hrothgar's feet, and through the bloodshed ran in hot pursuit, to track down she who came in vengeance.

To murder Grendel's mother.

On Beowulf ran, out into the depths of the Schrawynghop, and swift was she across the fen, and the trail she left was blood. The tracks took Beowulf down strange, forgotten paths, mile by mile, ending at the water's edge, beneath bog-trees that leant o'er hoar rock. There above the drop was the lunging warrior's head. His blood surged in the waters below.

Beowulf jumped.

Down he dived, and down, and all about him there were mere-wyrms and knuckers, things that thrust with tusk and maw – but Beowulf had battled foes as these since childhood, and many, many times on journeys into Geofon's domain. As he struck and sliced with Hrunting, of a sudden he felt a grip at his chest, and Grendel's mother bore him down, down, down to crushing depths – had not the mail shirt that he wore been that same Weyland-craft once worn by Wudga, her claws would surely then have skewered him, as all about the knuckers came to hew and strike once more.

Next Beowulf knew he was gulping air in some abysmal hall – a vaulted chamber deep beneath the wet, where burned strange fires for light – but the she-wolf was on him again, barrelling forward, tearing as she did, and Beowulf forced all his strength to his blade and struck her head with that fine Hrunting, ever-strong in battle.

The blade bounced off, and for the first time since before it was forged, it failed to kill an enemy.

She knocked him sprawling then, clattering to ground, and as he rolled Beowulf hurled that sword away to trust to his own hands, and leapt then onto her to wrassle, but he was held in turn and thrown himself, pinned down, as she astride him clambered, unsheathing her long knife and plunging it dead at his chest, and once again that Weyland saved his life.

On they grappled, she ever with the upper hand, and as they rolled and bucked on ground, Beowulf spied, about the dreary hall, amongst the treasures and debris, a blade gigantic and antique, edges stern with charms of victory – he twisted then, and as he lurched from under her he struck and knocked her down, then dove and grasped its hilt. In fierce mood and fell he hurled his force through that ring-adornéd blade, and at her neck it bitter seized – as she jerked and writhed, he plunged again, again, that ancient, entish blade, until he panting ceased, for she had been dead some time.

The sword was wet.

About him in the hall the fires blazed, and Beowulf sought Grendel then, and when he found the lifeless meat the sword did cleave that head asunder. The blade was seething now, as a branch thrust into fire, and it writhed and withered and was consumed, seemed to melt, then vanished like smoke in the air. Only the hilt remained in his hand.

High above the water-lair, Hrothgar and his court had likewise tracked, and stood about the water's edge now, mere-wyrms caught and dragged and killed upon the land. As all peered down, waiting, hungry there for tidings, the waters burst and boiled with blood, and there the gathered folk did bow their heads and weep for that great Beowulf, who gave his life that Heorot might once more be the hall that once it had.

As they fell to their knees in mourning, so then did Beowulf, swimming hard, appear before them – Hrunting strapped to his back, alongside Grendel's head and the entish hilt that yet remained. Hrothgar did rejoice, then, and grabbed him firm in embrace, tears in eyes.

Beowulf returned to his own land thereafter. Mighty were the treasures gifted him, and when Hygelac passed on to Woden's hall, Beowulf was king in his stead, and ruled fifty winters, and was loved.

Grendel's head was mounted in Heorot, then, high above the door, and men did look on it and marvel, and sing songs of Beowulf, and hope then to be better men.

The Desolation of Smeag

Far away from Beowulf's triumph, Hrothgar's kin, oblivious to all that was occurring back in Kent, were overseas, and once more begging Ingeld for his aid.

Bloated as now he was, Ingeld invited them, as always he did, to partake of the raucous feasting there for the sake of Freawaru, his wife, and to eat and drink their fill and then to eat and drink some more, and to taste what further pleasures they could find. This was the only aid he was willing to offer, but he hoped that it would satisfy, and that evening all fell to magnificent feast.

The elf-bright Freawaru then, gold-adorned, who though long in marriage now still shone as beautiful as one betrothed, traversed the floor whilst music played, enheartening young warriors with golden rings, bearing the goblet of ale to all good men in turn.

All was happiness, and glee.

But so too, in this fateful thirteenth year, a grim old warrior wandered back to that hall, the very hall where once he had served Frodo, his king, and how and when he entered nobody entirely knew.

And when he found it rich with smell and laughter, he found himself harden in disgust.

And when he saw the flesh of Freawaru, that daughter of the Scylding's who wore Frodo's gold and bounty, he found his chest to boil.

And when he saw her kin at highest table, and recognised on them the gleam of things prized by his sires of old – saw there a stout sword, ring-adorned, once treasure of a soldier he had known, chopped down by Scylding troops – then he gripped the table in his rage, and drank deep of the ale, and searched for a certain young man of the Heathobards.

'Canst thou not, my lord, the sword recall which thy father bore? His prizéd blade?' He gave the young man more to drink, pointed out which of the Scylding visitors now held it. 'Unto the fray he bore that blade, wore his visored helm that day whereon they slew him, the eager Scyldings, and were masters of the stricken field. Now here the sons of those same slayers walk this very hall, boasting of the prize and of the slaying of its owner, and wearing treasures which thou should'st by birthright still possess.'

He gave the young man another drink.

About the tables then that night the old man stalked, whispering in ears, penetrating conversation, creeping in amongst the benches, sowing his discord. Starting fires of hate. At each occasion there he stirred remembrance, prompted wounding words, until the hour came when all were deep in drink and hurt.

The old man rose, and slammed his sword upon the table.

Silence reigned.

The grim old warrior spoke.

'I came to find the son of Frodo, but I sought a brave man – I have come to a glutton. Who could have borne to take gold in ransom for a parent's death, or to have asked for gifts to atone for his father's murder? Why vex me with insolent gaze, you who honours the foe guilty of your father's blood, who takes his vengeance with loaves and warm soup? We burn with shame, thy people, lamenting thy infamies. I would crave no greater blessing, Frodo, if I might see those guilty of thy murder duly punished for such a crime!'

The hall was silent.

Ingeld's men began to nod. Began to stand. Began to shout.

Ingeld, weak and scared and eager to please, did as he was bid. Poured the whole flood of his anger and his fear on those at table with him, unsheathed his sword upon the kin of Freawaru with bloody ruthlessness, and there the Scyldings slept, red from bite of sword; their lives forfeit for their fathers' deeds.

And Ingeld looked to Freawaru, and Ingeld looked to the grim old warrior, and Ingeld looked to the men who filled the hall. He saw which way they leant. Ingeld stripped his wife then of riches and finery and banished her to the wilderness to die.

But Freawaru was not lost.

For though she'd led a life of luxury, she also had her father's mind. She travelled then in secret, back to Harty, and soon after Beowulf had left its shores she landed with her own companions, and made to Heorot straightway, to warn her father of the fighting force that even now prepared to march.

Hrothgar, strong once more within his purged and golden hall, commanded men to ready for war.

Hrothulf there did stand, that faithful nephew of Hrothgar whose parents both were kin to him, and took his place as battle-leader, honoured amongst the Scyldings. When Ingeld's men did come in waves and crash upon the Kentish shore, they all were met with blade and spear, and blood did fill the Schrawynghop once more, and knuckers feasted on the flesh of foe.

When the last battle came, as it had for Finn, it came with Ingeld entering the hall – he'd separated from the troops at shore, and made his way direct to Heorot, and there he sought to slay the ancient, noble Hrothgar, and there he stood, young still and strong, and there the old man battled once again, and as that Hrothulf crept into the hall, King Hrothgar won the day, and held that Ingeld at his knees, and there at spearpoint the glutton did submit to Hrothgar and to Hrothulf, and Hrothgar was appeased.

But Hrothulf, Hrothgar's kin, was not.

Hrothulf snatched the spear then from the king and plunged it through the throat of kneeling Ingeld. He took up Ingeld's sword then, and as that ancient Hrothgar castigated him he let the blade bite at his neck, and Hrothgar died betrayed, confused, reddening the floor's mosaic.

Hrothulf took the kingship then, master of Heorot thereafter.

But Hrothulf was not satisfied.

Soon both of Hrothgar's sons were dead, and none seemed quite to know the cause.

As Hrothulf sat in Hrothgar's gilded hall, Wealhtheow the wife of Hrothgar did mourn, and Wealhtheow did rage. And Hrothulf swore that he'd never be usurped as master of that hall.

So Wealhtheow journeyed then, and sought the son of honourable Heorogar, brief king before wise Hrothgar. She found this son, who was as noble as his father, and told him of the treachery of Hrothulf. Heoroweard was the name of this honourable man, and he marched then to press his claim for Hrothgar's hall.

Battle, then, raged on. The flames of hate burned hot.

All found an end when, as with Hnaef before him, Hrothulf barricaded, at the last, himself within the walls of Heorot – food enough to outlast any siege, and weapons to defend. Day waned, night fed. Heoroweard, then, did bellow in to him, 'Hrothulf, with your father's ruthlessness you win your hall. I give up my claim to it. Heorot is yours.'

As Hrothulf then alone rejoiced, the blaze of torches could be seen through richly laden windows. Though it was deep in night, red light shone, and men could be heard outside the thick, wooden door. It was not the dawn, nor a dragon flying past.

The gables of Heorot were aflame.

Amongst the ashes that were left next day, those of Hrothulf were indistinguishable from those of his precious hall.

The hate-flames did consume that day, and did rage on, long after they had been extinguished, and deep within the Schrawynghop that flame set fire to Grendel's hate, long since freed from body, and burned beneath the ken of man.

Across the waters, Beowulf reigned then as king, a happy and a fruitful time. Still as he aged he mourned for youth, and ached for battle and adventure once again. So it was that, when Beowulf was old and white, a halfling thief came running, dishevelled, to his hall, telling tales of a dragon deep, who dwelt upon an endless hoard of gathered gold and ancient jewels. He showed them there the finely wrought and gem-encrusted goblet he had taken as a proof.

The fire did reach him then, that Beowulf, long after it was set.

The dragon, outraged at the theft, began to burn the land and did destroy all Beowulf had forged and built and cared for in his reign.

But Beowulf did glee.

For once again he had the chance to taste adventure, once again the hope to die in battle, to Waelcyrge-ride to Woden's hall. He took a handpicked band, though when they reached a barrow near the lair commanded them to wait and offer aid when called upon and not before, for he must face the dragon first alone.

He found, of course, this age-old man grown soft on throne, the dragon was too much for him by far, and as he called his men they watched the devastation and they fled. Beowulf fought on, alone.

One fleeing man felt shame in mod too great, and turned then to rejoin – his name was Wiglaf, and he came too late to save King Beowulf, but rallied just in time to help destroy the wyrm.

He fell there, Beowulf. His foe slain, fires all about. In his hands he gazed at golden treasure from the hoard, so ancient and so beautiful that as he died he smiled.

Beowulf was placed upon a pyre, in time, and there the flames consumed, and his glory departed. The fire of hate that started in the Schrawynghop, so long ago, flared and died then too. That creeping, penetrating, subtle fire of hate and cunning, which we call smeag. Beowulf's remains were buried in a mound, high on the cliff, with all the useless gold that he had won.

The time of Beowulf was past.

Bretwalda
The Age of
England

The Bretwalda, or Britain-Wielder, is precisely that. An Anglo-Saxon king who held dominion over the bulk of Britain, who could wield the land in its entirety, and who held the many peoples within it under his sway. The Bretwalda is the Anglo-Saxon precursor to the King of all England, and the incipient beginning of a single, inclusive, united English identity – one that puts nation before tribe, and cohesion before division.

The
Beginning
of Wonders

So it was, that in AD 495 there came two leaders into Britain, Cerdic and Cynric, with five ships, at a place then known as Cerdic's-ore, which we today call Charford, in the Ytene Forest. Cerdic was an Englishman, and Cerdic was a Briton. His great-grandfather was Giwis, founder of the Anglo-Saxon Gewisse tribe; his British mother had been Belgic royalty, and knew the cruelty of Natanleod well.

Like Wurtgern before him, King Natanleod (or Netley, as we say) was a weak and selfish man who kept a weak and selfish crowd about him. The land around the south coast was his domain.

The land deserved better.

When word of the ships came to that king, it came in the middle of a meal. Happily stewing in mead and in meat, surrounded by his court of sycophants, Netley was outraged at the disturbance, spilling drink and platter alike as he raged at the messenger.

'Tell this half-breed that the land and those who squat on it are mine and mine alone, to use and do with as I please, and it pleases me not to have his filth infecting it. He has until the morning light to flee the way he came or on to other lands, else we shall meet in battle, and his blood I will use to water the ground, and his bones to feed the earth, and his head to adorn my hall.'

The messenger rode to Cerdic's encampment, to pass on the drunken challenge. There he was welcomed with forbearance, and Cerdic listened to his words in silence, as the voice of the nervous rider recounted the sorts of insults that only a man who won't have to deliver them himself would choose.

Once it was over, Cerdic simply nodded, thanked the messenger for his service, and bid him wait nearby, with food and drink and fresh hay for his horse, until the response was ready to send.

When the messenger returned to Netley, he did so with a gift for his king; the sheath of Cerdic's sword, and the promise that Cerdic would take it back himself when it was needed once more.

Thus the war began.

For thirteen years skirmishes and petty conflict roiled and yawed between Cerdic's people and Netley's, and Cerdic's blade remained unsheathed and bloody. The great reckoning promised by Netley had not followed on from the message he sent. He'd responded, instead, with a force of half-cocked fighters, unprepared. The men that came were killed, or were stripped of their weapons and armour, and sent back barefoot.

Netley's manoeuvres since had been intermittent bursts of violence and hostility, alternated with frantic, obsessive devotion to his personal defences. The farms and settlements of his people were left to their own devices, and to the mercy of Cerdic.

For thirteen years, then, this state of gradual gnawing and general anxiety pervaded, as Cerdic's camp within the Ytene rooted and his followers grew, joined by local Jutes and Belgae, and others from across the seas.

Soon enough, Cerdic's Ytene grew to reflect Cerdic himself, as the Belgae and the Jutes, the Celtic and the Anglo-Saxon, the British of England and the English of Britain, grew to live and think and be as one – as kinsmen and as comrades in arms against the tyranny of old King Netley.

Finally, in AD 508, the two armies met full in the field for a decisive, final battle; a battle for the Ytene, for the Gewisse, and for the future of their peoples. Netley could stand to lose no more in dribs and drabs to the burgeoning realm of Cerdic – if he was weakened any further he would inevitably be crushed. He knew his only hope was one last, desperate, all-or-nothing assault on a looming future that threatened no place for him.

Netley's chosen ground was that below his hill-fort, which we today call Tatchbury Mount, where he called in favours and debts and mercenaries from all over Britain and beyond, accruing a vast horde of over ten thousand fighters for his cause.

Some say Netley invoked ancient alliances that day, and strange pacts. That ettins and gigans and inhuman forces swelled his terrible ranks.

Though they were strong fighters, Cerdic knew that in pitched battle against Netley's unnatural army his likelihood of victory was narrow. Heavily outnumbered, his only hope was tactical, and though his advisors baulked at depleting their already limited numbers, he nevertheless divided his forces in two; a right flank and a left.

Cerdic was to lead the stronger and more experienced right flank himself, made up of the three thousand men who had sailed with him thirteen years earlier, whilst Cynric was to lead the left, comprising those who had joined in the intervening years – Jutes and Gewisse, Belgae, British and English alike.

The morning of the battle came, and Netley stepped from the hill-fort to survey his troops. An impressive sight they were. Obedient men, cruel men, ruthless men; he had them all, and more besides – the strange, bloated, towering things from deep within the woods; the squat ones with flashing eyes from out of the barrows; the twisted, staring things he didn't like to watch.

He looked at his instruments of victory, and he felt triumph. Thirteen years of humiliation, of ignominy, of insult. Soon he would be revenged upon them all, and have all that was rightfully his once more. His land. His people. His right.

They all belonged to him.

As Netley paced about he felt a crunch beneath his foot, looked down and smeared the remains of a beetle on the wet grass. He continued on his way, stepping more carefully than before, admiring the exotic array of strange armours and unfamiliar blades, until he came to a small, muddy stream of stagnant water, and turned away to avoid the smell.

As he retraced his route, Netley passed a bent and blackened tree he had not noticed before. An old man lay beneath it, dead or dying. Netley strode on, avoiding eye contact, back to his hill-fort, head swelling with dreams of dominance and glory.

Far away, Cerdic paced about the heathland. Looked to the swelling, distant sight of the enemy at the hill. Cerdic turned and walked in a different direction, searching for peace from the rising tide of thought. He walked, and he walked, and before he knew it he could look about him and see nothing but the boundless land, and hear nothing but the song of the birds and the whip of the wind, and smell only pollen and earth. He stood and he breathed, and felt the silence of the landscape fold about him.

Cerdic sank to the floor, first sitting, then lying in the rough tapestry of grass and ground, weed and lichen. He shut his eyes and breathed deep the earth. He spoke, there and then, unashamed and open, prayed to the land that enwrapped him, to the Ytene itself. He felt the cool dew wet on his face, and the softness of the grass. He opened his eyes.

Inches from his nose was a stag beetle, upturned amongst the green blades and caught on its back, wiry legs fighting at air, pincers twisting. Cerdic gently righted the beetle, who disappeared into the rough green of the ground.

'You, at least, survive this day, my friend,' Cerdic said.

He heaved himself to standing. There, in the peace of that forest heathland, he felt the landscape about him like a blanket or a cloak. He walked there, safe, until he came to a little stream dammed by a fallen tree, with a tiny colony of half-dead water creatures, gaping helpless, trapped in the dried-up patch that once had been safe and wet and full of life.

Cerdic moved aside the fallen tree and cleared the clumps of leaf and bracken, watching the water fill their home once more as the vigour of the animals returned, and he smiled to see the stream returned to health.

'You, at least, survive this day, my friends.'

Cerdic watched the waters there until he didn't, and walked on, and came to the start of a path, next to which was a twisted, blackened tree, claw-branches spreading wide. Beneath it an old, old man lay, broken and wounded. Cerdic knelt beside him.

The man was older than any he had known.

His bulging eyes were pale and almost white, his skin the same. Wrinkled with age beyond imagination, bruised about his throat, and in his side a gaping wound. From his head there curled two horns, curven like a ram's, matching the upturned ends of the thick, white moustache that sat above the beardless but unshaven jaw. Cerdic put his ear to the old man's chest and felt the faintest of somethings. Life clung still.

Cerdic dressed the old man's wound, poured water from the nearby stream between his cracked lips. The old man blinked, heaved himself to sitting, the wrinkles filling before Cerdic's eyes. As he rose, weakness and age receding, the bulging eyes glowed strangely, and they looked into Cerdic's own and they gripped his mind and they gripped his mod, and the old man opened his mouth and spoke words in a language both strange and familiar, which Cerdic could not understand but felt he knew.

And then the old man was gone.

Cerdic tried and failed to speak. Where the man had been Cerdic saw an axe, rusted in the earth. He picked up the tool from the ground, cleaned it as best he could, and attacked the roots of the tree. He hacked and he hewed, he chopped and he heaved, and after what could have been an hour and could have been a lifetime, the dark and black and twisted wood collapsed to earth, its trunk laid low, hollow with decay – a single fresh, white shoot now visible in the wound.

Cerdic walked away, and followed the path to battle.

A wolf watched, silent in the trees.

The day wore on, the armies marched, and the killing began. Seeing his divided foe, Netley sent the full force of his rage to the right flank, to Cerdic, whose blood he vowed would water the ground, whose bones would feed the earth, whose head would decorate his hall. Skulls were crushed, then, and limbs were torn and life spilled out from dying men, and things that were not men hallooed and screamed, and darkest deeds were done, and Cerdic's forces then were driven back.

As Cerdic's flank retreated, Netley watched and smiled. For a flicker of an instant he considered just allowing them escape, lives and shame intact. But Netley had made his vow, and knew he would never be satisfied but by blood, by bones, and by the utter desolation of his enemy. He commanded pursuit, he commanded slaughter, and his forces obeyed.

On they galloped, but as Cerdic's flank fell back and drew them on, Cynric's wheeled to pursue, enveloping and surrounding Netley's forces, sending waves of panic and confusion as renewed attack came from behind, just as they thought to find resistance quenched.

At this, Cerdic's men rallied and turned with second vigour, and Netley's forces found onslaught from all sides, chaos swirling through them, and no way to retreat to advantageous ground.

The tide of battle began to turn.

Cerdic himself pressed through the maelstrom, hacking and roaring as he did, until the flight of a raven overhead caught his eye, and he watched it score the horizon, where the distant figure of an old man stood, with curven horns like those of a ram. Though he was far away, Cerdic heard him speak as clearly as a whisper in the ear – the same familiar words from when they first had met. Though still the words he spoke were strange, and in a language Cerdic did not know, now Cerdic understood them, every one:

'You, at least, survive this day, my friend.'

As he watched, the old man lifted his arms and the ground beneath the warring men began to shift, to flow, and from the centre of Netley's ranks great, liquid trees shot up, crushing and hurling and impaling men as they did so. From amongst the panicked warriors the ettins and the gigans turned on those about them, started fighting against Netley's troops from within. Chaos reigned. An eagle circled, cackling and impatient, and Netley watched horrified as his army collapsed, begging for the mercy of Cerdic.

Netley fled.

He ran, cowardly, from his hill-fort, alone to the marshy ground below, stained red with the blood of the fallen – ran as far from those still left alive as his feet allowed, ran until he felt a crunch in the ground, and looked down to see that all was blackness.

The earth he stood on was alive.

Countless beetles, over feet, up leg, inside his clothes – coating him, weighing him down. Still, he tried to run, but the soil started to give, the reddened mud parting to muck and stagnant, bloody swamp.

He looked to the sky and screamed for help, called to the lone figure of an old man in the distance. An old man with bulging eyes that avoided his, an upward-curled moustache, and curven horns like those of a ram.

The bulging eyes turned, filled Netley's soul; stared through and into and beyond him, and the old man spoke in strange and unfamiliar words, in a language Netley could not understand and never would.

Netley watched in gaping silence as, from the blood-marsh beneath, the bones of dead men rose to drag him down into the forest floor, skeletal fingers clawing cold and strong, his own lich army pulling him down, down, to lead them in eternity.

When Cerdic's men had won the day, the rest of Netley's forces had surrendered, and the dead men had been counted, all that could be found of Netley was his head – no body beneath it, upright in the bloodied earth of the marsh – gaping silent at something no living man could see. In the empty hill-fort of Tatchbury Mount, Cerdic found the sheath of his sword.

He wiped the blood from his blade, and returned it to its home to rest.

Cerdic, then, ruled the Ytene, which today we call the New Forest, and in this soil he planted his roots and strengthened his forces, gradually increasing his land, until the territory of the Gewisse spread through much of the south. He took the island of Vectis a few years later, gifting it to his nephews Stuf and Wihtgar (after whom it was renamed as the Isle of Wiht). To the old warrior Port and his sons, Bieda and Maegla, Cerdic gifted land around what now is Portchester, for they had served him well, and given two ships of fighting men when most he needed it.

Thus the kingdom of Wessex was founded.

Cerdic named that baleful battleground the Netley Marsh and, rather than display the head of his vanquished foe in triumph, he took the trophy and rode just beyond the bounds of the Ytene, near to a village named Downton. There he had the head buried in a mound facing away from the Forest, to ward off any future foe. The mound was after known as Nettlebury, and survives there still.

Over five thousand dead men fed the New Forest that day, alongside their petty King Netley, and it is said that at certain times of twilight and the year, in what they named the lich-moor, and what we call the Latchmore Brook, travellers who know how can gaze to the marshy ground below and see the lich army submerged beneath, the gaping faces of long-dead soldiers floating by, whispering things in languages familiar and strange.

Some say they've seen a headless lich amongst the rest, in raiment fit for a king, who beckons to those who stare, and stretches out his arms to them.

I have seen no such thing myself, and nothing you can do will make me look.

The Revenging of Arilda

Oh maid, whose bones in Gloucester rest, by whom all Gloucester folk are blessed – three times she fought the power of sin, and joined the land, made pure within.

Once upon a time, in what today we call Gloucestershire, there lived a woman named Arilda.

This Arilda not only was a fierce and mighty beauty, but also was a fierce and mighty fighter – a battle-maiden – flesh unstained and pure of mind.

She'd made a vow on her arrival in Britain that she would take no husband, know no carnal love, until her battles all were fought, and a lasting home built for her people, safe and sound. That the man she would take would be he who was worthy of her, and worthy of her land.

On this vow she had a golden ring forged, the ring of her people, which held their mark. This ring she swore she'd give unto the man she chose, and not to any other. This perfect, pure and golden thing was her very self, and had her power invested in it.

But Arilda was a beautiful woman, as beautiful as she was fierce (and fierce she was, indeed), and there were many who desired her, many too who sought her as a prize, and many still who did not care to meet her standards. Many had tried to take her, and had tried to take her golden ring, and many had been killed so doing, and not a single one attempting it had ever there succeeded.

In time, and tentatively, the great and fierce and beautiful Arilda let it be known she sought the man who was her match, a man of greater worth than even she could ever be.

The first who came before her was a beauty indeed, with high cheekbones and thick hair, broad shoulders and snake hips. A man who never had known what it was to not be lusted over, and who never had to know.

When this elf-bright man stood pouting there before her, Arilda bid him tell her of his worth, and he described the beauty she could see, and told of all the countless others who had worshipped at his face, and of the countless more who longed there for his touch. He told her all of this, and Arilda with disdain told him to leave.

The suitor gaped.

Never in his life had shining beauty been rejected. Head reeling, soon it settled into fear, and soon it rose to anger, and the suitor lunged forth to take what he knew to be his. Before he felt it, a sword had uglied his beautiful face, and Arilda stood battle-swollen and panting above, bloody and fine and fierce.

Time passed, and another suitor came, and when he did, he did so in style. Before him in procession came acrobats and musicians, dancers and gleemen – all singing songs of him and his greatness.

Amongst his courtiers she recognised the scarred face of her former suitor, still dainty and beautiful in flesh, but cowed now, insecure, and ugly for it. His pride shattered, he hurried after the man who bought his services, who swelled with the boldness that once had been his. Carried aloft, the new suitor was, in a great and richly fitted train, and when he emerged before Arilda he did so dripping with finely wrought gold, priceless jewels and treasures from across the Middle Earth.

When the rich man stood before her, Arilda bid him tell her of his worth, and he described his riches, and told of all the countless others he had bought and sold, and the worlds that he could move with wealth alone, of the things that he could own, of the infinity of power it gave him – and the pampering and lazy pleasure it was in his gift to give. He told her all of this, and Arilda with disdain told him to leave.

The suitor was struck dumb.

Never in his life had the glister of gold been rejected. Head reeling, soon it settled into fear, and soon it rose to anger, and so the suitor lunged to take what he knew to be his. Before he felt it, a sword had torn the treasures and silks from his body, and sent him naked on his way. Arilda stood battle-swollen behind, bloody and beautiful and fierce.

Time passed and another suitor came, by name of Municus, and the floor shook and the walls shuddered. On his palanquin were hoist the skulls and fleshen heads of vanquished foes, and they were many. Amongst them Arilda recognised the faces of her former suitors, saw glints of gold and statuary that once had belonged to the man who'd preceded him.

When he stood before her, Arilda bid him tell her of his worth, and he spoke of his battles, of the countless peoples he had slain, of the death and destruction he had wrought, and the armies he'd lain waste to with his sword. He told her all of this, and Arilda with disdain told him to leave.

The suitor stared, cold.

'You seek a man to overpower you. I am he. Strong and fierce you may well be, but none are stronger than I. None can battle well as I. None can stand before my blade.'

'You are weak. Too weak for life with me.'

'I have killed gods and monsters, slaughtered ettins and murdered ents. I have defeated thyrs and extinguished dragon, caught knucker and nix and hung them to dry. I have razed cities to the ground, and pulled the very mountains to the floor. There is no king, no nation on the Middle Earth that does not know my name and fear it. Who are you to call me weak?'

'I seek a man with strength enough to build.'

Municus was silenced.

Never in his life had any rejected his strength. With a roar, and axe in hand, Municus charged, and there the warriors fought, and Arilda was defeated, and Municus stripped her and pushed her to her knees, and meant to take her then.

Arilda knew she could not hope to kill the beast that towered over her, but knew that she could leave a wound. So as the suitor lunged to take what he knew to be his, and before he knew an attack was left, the battle-maiden, not quite defeated, had torn with nail and tooth between his legs, and turned him to a gelding.

In disbelieving roar of pain and shame he swung his axe, and took the head from off Arilda's shoulders, too late, and as it flew through the air Arilda's head did laugh and laugh, and laughter echoed high about the land, a laugher at the man she had unmanned; the triumph of the battle-maiden.

Where her laughing head came down, the goddess Geofon in praise of her sent forth a stream, and water flowed, and the sound of the current was laughter, and it rang through Municus's ears. On Arilda's naked, headless body, the golden ring of her vow shone bright and pure.

From that day forward, though Municus survived, it was no life. His pride shattered, he soon became a mockery of men, and though he still had strength in arms, he could not lead an army, or inspire dryht.

Municus went wreccan then, and travelled through the Middle Earth to find a place where none knew of his shame, but found it only where no others dwelt. Even in those lonely lands, wherever water was, he heard the laughter of Arilda fill his ears.

The tribe that was Arilda's was called Hwicce, and the land their own. Though many warred for it, and briefly held and quickly lost it, it would take generations until the Hwicce found a kingdom worthy of joining.

In AD 577, Ceawlin of Wessex fought and won and occupied, at the Battle of Deorham. But occupation is not submission, as Arilda knew. After the Battle of Fethanleag, where his son was slain, Ceawlin departed the land. Unsatisfied.

It wasn't until another generation came, and that great King of the Mark, Penda, who we shall speak of soon, battled hard with Wessex at Cirencester and, in 628, the victory was his. He did not occupy or force himself upon the Hwicce, but rather through alliance they did join, retaining each identity but growing closer, in shared partnership.

So it was, they say, that Penda swam the River Severn, and sought out the waters of Arilda, and when he heard her laughter he swam deep, and deep, on and in to the sacred vessel, and there in Geofon's domain Arilda bid him tell her of his worth, and he told her simply that he recognised hers, and trusted that she recognised his, without the need of words or tricks or flattery.

Penda found exposed then, there, in the wet, the pure and golden ring that was Arilda's vow, and she let him take it, and he wore it on him ever after.

Arilda still appears today, head and sword in hand, at the holy well that bears her name, in the hamlet we call Kington, where waters run red with her blood. Her bones were shared between two churches, one her head, at Oldbury-on-Severn, and one her body, in Oldbury-on-the-Hill, both of which bear her name and pray to her, and have for many centuries. Her remains were later moved from Oldbury-on-the-Hill to Gloucester Abbey, though the hand which had borne her golden ring remained. Her abbey shrine is long since destroyed, her newest tomb unmarked.

But in Gloucestershire, the Hwicce remember her still.

The
Altars of
Raedwald

Once upon a time, there were three English kings.

These three English kings worshipped the Allruler above all else, and were the first of the English kings to do so.

First of the three was Ethelbert, King of Kent, third of the great Bretwaldas, who deep into his reign received the rite of baptism, and did so for love of Bertha, his wife, who long had placed the Allruler highest. Under his reign two further kings converted: first Saebert, King of Essex, then Raedwald, King of East Anglia.

Ethelbert and Saebert both worshipped hard this Gloryfather, and urged on all about them to do likewise, and rejected those who did not. So it was, the most ambitious of their courts did join them, and the worst of men were encouraged in conversion, whilst the best found such divisiveness distasteful, and kept to their familiar course.

Ethelbert was powerful, and did much good, but he was blinded by his faith, and Saebert also. Both prioritised the trappings of their church above the merits of their men, and both prioritised the bonds of their new god over those of family. Both forgot the value of that which came before, and both forgot to give their kin the legacy and leadership that was their birthright.

In AD 616 both died.

Ethelbert's throne passed to his son, one Eadbald, who, now his father was departed, felt such freedom from the cloying, draining weight of him that he rejoiced – and as he had been given nothing of his father's love, for all had gone to Gloryfather high, Eadbald did reject that which he did resent.

This Eadbald then renounced his baptism, and lived in the manner of his forefathers, scorning the Allruler and all who kept to him.

Eadbald grew wild.

His first act on taking the throne of his father was to take the wife of his father, who found that she enjoyed the younger man by far, rather than the old and pious, pompous one who'd married her when still she was a child.

They had two sons, who we shall speak of later.

* * *

Saebert, on the other hand, had not one son, not two, but three – two of whom, Sexred and Saeward, took the kingship jointly. His sons had never been baptised, and so had never taken on their father's god to be rejected. With their self-involved and arrogant parent gone, they proudly, openly, did serve their gods once more, who long had been restrained.

In both Kent and Essex, then, the people who had thus far had to keep their ancient faith held secret, did rejoice. For far too long the old, familiar ways were scorned by their elite who, high in halls of privilege, indulged in new and fashionable ideals which spread across the world and overrode all native custom, which held no place for humble or old-fashioned folk – mocked for looking backwards, to the values of the ones who came before.

In both kingdoms, then, the people and their fresh young rulers did embrace with relish and with heartiness all that had been disdained and held from them, and did so with more glee and vigour than they ever would have had they not been scorned, and had their kings been moderate, and had their lords allowed them just to hold their past without hostility or shame.

The third king, however – Raedwald, in East Anglia – still lived.

And he had found a different path.

For Raedwald, though he worshipped and acknowledged that ruler and great architect of all, did not deny the other gods that he had always known.

When Raedwald built his church, he had two altars in it: one to the new and triple god, above the rest, and one to all the others, to the fathers and the mothers who he and his people had always served, and always been served by in return.

Raedwald allowed and encouraged the folk to serve just as they pleased, and pray to whom they pleased, and do so how they pleased. He saw faith not in black and white, but many-coloured, many-hued. He saw the Gloryfather, high above, and saw as well great Woden, Tue and Thunner. Saw Frig and Hretha and Eostre. Let the people feed Erce, let them give to Geofon, let them wait for Ingui's return.

Raedwald understood that, no matter there how right and wise and widespread round the Middle Earth his new ideas might be, no matter how positive he thought his progress, he was but a man, and arrogance comes easy, safe in gilded halls. The ancient, cherished passions and traditions of his people all had value – even those he felt misguided, foolish or unhelpful. Even those he thought might be unkind, unwise.

Raedwald, in this way, lived long and fruitfully, and became the fourth Bretwalda. He let his people and his family embrace those elements of heritage they pleased, making sure to teach them all of it, and not to pick and choose, or to impose his preferences, or to unmake what always then had been.

Kent and Essex, soon, in wake of those selfish, pious, pompous rulers who cared not much for those who weren't their ilk in thought, fell hard to Wessex, and many people then were slaughtered. Never again would those realms have the strength that once they had.

East Anglia did thrive.

* * *

In years to come did Raedwald give a home to Edwin of Northumbria, in exile, fleeing from the great King Aethelfrith, who first ruled both the northern kingdoms of Deira and Bernicia, and so did first unite the North, and give a single throne to all Northumbria.

Edwin's father had been King of Deira, making Edwin a rival claimant for this northern throne. Edwin placed Ingui above all other gods, but gave the rest their due – it was, after all, as he honoured Eostre, that an assassin from Wessex had tried to pierce him with a venomous blade.

Whilst Edwin was sheltered in exile by Raedwald, Aethelfrith did all he could to convince the king to kill Edwin or hand him over – thrice offered riches, threatened war, urged him that this Edwin was inhuman, cruel and merciless – to kill such men was justice.

Raedwald, though, in his great realm, which did not see in black and white, disagreed. He saw a man as more than what he thought, and did not judge him by the words of his enemy, or even those he used himself. Nevertheless, the threats that Aethelfrith made were real, and gave him pause. As Raedwald pondered the safety of his people, and how to resolve his problem, Edwin awaited word of his decision with silent anguish through a sleepless night, sat outside on the steps to Raedwald's hall.

It was in this state, consumed with blinding fire, that Edwin received a strange and hooded visitor, tall and grim and old, at sight of whom, unknown and unlooked for, Edwin felt a terror deep within. The hooded stranger came close up, saluted him, and asked him why he sat in solitude on stone, troubled and wakeful when all were fast asleep.

'What is it to you whether I spend the night within doors or abroad?'

The stranger replied, 'Do not think that I am ignorant of the cause of your grief, your watching, and sitting alone without. For I know of a surety who you are, and why you grieve, and the evils that you fear will soon fall upon you. Tell me what reward you would give the man who should deliver you from these troubles, and persuade Raedwald neither to harm you himself, nor deliver you up to be murdered by others.'

Edwin replied that he would give such a one all that he could. The grim, hooded man then asked, 'What if he also assured you your enemies should be destroyed, and you should be a king surpassing in power, not only all your own ancestors, but even all that have reigned before in England?'

Edwin promised he would make a fitting return.

The old man spoke a third time.

'But if he who truly foretells these great blessings about to befall you could also give you better and more profitable counsel than any of your fathers or kindred ever heard, do you consent to submit to him, and to follow his guidance?'

Edwin promised.

Woden laid his right hand on Edwin's head. 'When this sign shall be given you, remember what has passed between us, and do not delay what you now promise.'

When he took his hand away, Edwin was alone.

Raedwald chose to protect Edwin.

There, without force, without distorted truths or hidden facts, did Edwin thrive, and of his own accord in that shared church he learned the Gloryfather's ways, and learned the open, even-handed ways of Raedwald too, the ways of the third of our three kings.

And Raedwald slew that Aethelfrith, and Edwin won once more his father's throne, and ruled in that united North, and did so married to a daughter of Ethelbert, that first of the three, and did so knowing of the

Allruler – knowing he rose high above the rest, but knowing that the rest had value, too.

And the altars of Raedwald, in his shared church, which kept a place always for what had been, and never was restricted to a single vision of what should someday be, stood there for many generations.

When Raedwald died, around 624, for his greatness and his wisdom his people gave the richest burial that any then had known. A huge and sweeping ship was there constructed, to serve him in the journey to Neorxnawang, filled with treasures and with precious things. With idols of the old gods and the new.

Some say, today, that this great burial is that of Sutton Hoo, and I've no reason to deny it.

Raedwald's son did take his kingship then. He ruled for as long as he embraced his father's open faith, though once he leaned too hard into divisive notions of one God alone, one right and many wrongs, he too was slain by his people, and for three years Woden ruled East Anglia once more.

But Edwin held true to the lessons of Raedwald, and was loved, and grew to be fifth of the great Bretwaldas, as his grim visitor had long ago foretold.

The path to take, should ever you have reason to choose, is always that of Raedwald. To do what you believe to be right, but always to allow that you might not be. To remember, always, that what you and what others know is very little, and the present time a very, very little one, in a vast and spreading past and future.

That though you may be very fine, with very many fond of you, you are only quite a little fellow in a wide world, after all.

And thank goodness, I say.

Penda's Grin

When Edwin received the sign of Woden, he received it from a Christian bishop.

Confused, he was, but had given his word to do as he was bid without question.

Could it be true that Woden urged him to baptism?

Edwin called a witan, then, and asked his wisest councillors their thoughts. All found it hard to scrutinise, for fearful were they either way to displease Woden. Finally, Edwin's old, familiar companion, Coifi, pulled back his hood and spoke.

'The god-craft we have hitherto preferred has no profit to it left. None have applied themselves more diligently than I, yet there are many now who receive greater favours, and are more preferred. I have seen another age, yet to come, in which dry bones will once again grow flesh, and wooden statuary will root and sprout to tree once more. My counsel is, O King, we sacrifice in fire those temples and those altars we have known. Who, more fittingly than myself, can destroy those things for example to all others, through the wisdom which has been given me?'

Coifi then commanded Edwin give him arms and a stallion, that he might mount and go forth to destroy the idols. Having girt a sword about him, with spear in hand, he mounted the king's stallion, and rode grimly to the square, where crowds in festival gave worship to Eostre.

The multitude, beholding him, saw mad-craft in his burning eye and knew him, and were afraid. He rode up to the shrine, then, and cast his spear deep into it, and flames then did devour, and down it crumbled, and Coifi did ride over it and on.

This mound now holds a Christian church on it – All Hallows, in Goodmanham, half a day's ride east of York, beyond the River Derwent.

It was only much later that Edwin remembered he did not know Coifi at all, and realised that Coifi had never before been a member of the witan, though he felt as familiar as a childhood friend. No other that he asked could answer him.

Edwin met Coifi at least once more.

Edwin then had long been warring with the Welsh, and had defeated them full many, many times. The king of Gwynedd, then, in northern Wales, was Cadwallon ap Cadfan. Cadwallon knew the blade of Edwin, and had lost to him before. Cadwallon knew he needed an alliance.

Cadwallon was a Christian, and a Briton.

Penda was neither.

But Penda, with his vow to the land and his golden ring, understood the Raedwaldian way, and had no prejudice against the Welsh, and had no prejudice against worship of the Gloryfather that did not preclude his own. Penda had no difficulty in joining forces with Cadwallon, and Cadwallon had no difficulty allowing Penda his own worship, his own magic, and his own gods.

So it was, at the Battle of Hatfield Chase in 633, that this alliance rose against King Edwin of Northumbria, and many thyrs fought there that day, and many magics and much hagcraft rose. Strange things reigned on that bloody field, things that could not be explained or countered by the men who allowed for none but the Allruler's way. As wolf howled was Woden seen with spear, as eagle cried was Tue with sword, as raven croaked did Waelcyrge ride hard above the battlefield, and in thunderous crash did Thunner and Dinne cross the skies, as Heofenfyr struck down and Edwin's ranks were decimated.

Edwin there, on that strange field, saw grim old Coifi ride up on the stallion he'd taken long before. He saw the hooded face and burning eye, and saw the spear that flew to him, and opened up his mind, and hollowed out his skull. Osfrith, his eldest son, was struck down also in the field – his youngest, Eadfrith, was taken still-living by Penda, and sacrificed after battle to the oldest gods that Penda knew.

Northumbria was then divided, once more. Eanfric, son of Aethelfrith, returned from exile to rule Bernicia, whilst Edwin's cousin Osric took on Deira's throne. The Gloryfather, then, was renounced in the North. When Osric rose against Cadwallon, he too was slain. His brother Oswald, wreccan in what now is eastern Scotland, then travelled home to take the throne.

In time, Oswald rose and did defeat Cadwallon, and reunite the north at the Battle of Heavenfield, only to later fall to Penda's forces. For many winter's, then, was Penda's Mercia most powerful of all the Seven Kingdoms.

For Penda, though as vigorous a worshipper of Woden as he was a warrior, did not have enmity to any gods, and did not seek to alter any from their paths. He did allow the spear-blind head of Edwin to be taken

to York, and to the church of Peter the Apostle, where it was revered, and given proper rites. And perhaps this was Penda's weakness.

For just as honour alone is little strength against dishonourable foes, beliefs that allow the beliefs of others will always be vulnerable to those that do not, for they provide sanctuary to the very enemies that seek to destroy them.

Soon enough, Penda was alone amongst the Seven Kings of England in rejecting the dominance of the Allruler. In this new and lonely world Penda trusted too, too well that old alliances, and ancient favours done, would hold a loyalty that then was out of fashion.

At the Battle of Winwaed, Penda lead another great alliance against the forces of Bernicia. The King of Gwynedd, then, battle-shirker, abandoned him. The King of Deira fled and stayed safe on his royal fence. Penda, abandoned by all but East Anglia, was slain that day.

From thereon in, the kings of Mercia placed the Gloryfather above all others, his might in their eyes proven. All the Seven Kings of all the Seven Kingdoms held, thereafter, unstinting to his worship, and never more did they return to the worship of their great, shared ancestor (though scatterings of minor tribal kingdoms held out longer).

Some say that he was old, by then, was Penda, and grim-visaged. A man well into his eighties, who had ruled wide for over thirty winters.

They say that on the battlefield that day old Penda strode about, no mortal getting near him, slaying all with ease but, looking hard and seeing not an ally in sight, they say that Penda felt sore old, and lost his faith in men, and changing worlds, and slaughtered gods.

They say that Penda looked up, then, into the face of Coifi, who pulled back his hood and was Woden. Told him that his fight was done, his sacrifice was made. That all was as it should be, his place at table earned. Showed him all that there was planned, and let him taste the mad-craft that would make it all make sense.

They say that when his corpse was found, on either side there perched a bird – a raven and an eagle who whispered secrets in his ears of all that was to come, and all that yet had been. King Penda simply lay there, dead.

A smile upon his old and pristine face.

The Rumwold Prophecy

When Penda died, much changed.

The children of Penda were many, and vigorous. Though all in time acknowledged the Allruler's lordship over Woden, this did not happen overnight.

Cyneburh was a bold and brazen girl, beautiful and strong, and as unrelenting as her great father had been. She grew to be a lusty woman, who knew what she wanted, and was willing to do what it took to get it.

When she first met Alhfrith, she knew what it was that she wanted.

Alhfrith was King Oswiu's eldest son, that same Oswiu who would, soon after, defeat Penda in battle at the Winwaed, and in so doing rise to prominence, as the seventh of the great Bretwaldas. This had not yet come to pass, however, and it was in the interests of all to try, through such a marriage, to weave a peace between their houses.

Cyneburh was hungry through the wedding, and hungry through the wedding feast, and hungry when that night they took to bed.

With relish, then, she watched her fresh and still-green husband stand before her, and with relish she watched as he removed the raiment of the day, and with relish she watched as he entered their bed.

Then he bid her sweet dreams, and fell fast asleep.

Cyneburh was restless that night.

And so she was the next night, and the night after that.

This was not what Cyneburh thought marriage to be.

Finally, hungry as she'd ever been and mad with frustration, she roared at her fresh husband, demanding why he would not satisfy her.

He, surprised, had thought she knew. He placed the Gloryfather above all things, and above all gods, and could not lie with any woman who did not.

Cyneburh submitted to the Allruler then, unsure entirely what that meant, and Alhfrith submitted to the marital bed.

And Cyneburh was satisfied thereafter.

She became pregnant, in time, and it was whilst journeying through Mercia that labour started. In a pleasant field, then, filled with lilies and roses, servants and soldiers eagerly spread out the camp and the tents, and soon this royal Cyneburh gave birth by the side of the road.

But as the babe was born, from out between her legs his shapeless cries on hitting air became full words, and so the freshly minted voice began to speak – head swivelling from father to mother and screaming out, endlessly, 'Am I Christian!? Am I Christian!?'

Once the boy had filled his mouth with teat and drunk, he found some other words to say, and spoke them fluidly but strange, as if he sought to fill each second up with sentiment.

'I know of many gods, I hold full many memories, I know and am each worshipper and every priest, and high above them all does stand the Master Builder, and I do know of him as I do know all things in Middle Earth. I am Rumwold – and as I have but little time remaining, and too little far to give to every undergod, I must trust myself to the care of the Allruler, and be baptised as Rumwold in his name.'

At this all gaped, and fell to their knees.

Child Rumwold then was baptised – and speedily. Cyneburh tried to make it a royal affair, and grand as she had known such ceremonials to be, but Rumwold refused, demanding only the humblest of rites, instructing them to walk a certain route, and to beg whatever wanderers they found there to come and perform the ritual, for these men, though rough and wild, would have the knowledge needed. Alhfrith had sent for a vessel of water to carry out the christening, but Rumwold screamed no, and instead pointed to a distant hut in a spread of fen and marshland, known to be haunted by strange, unfriendly things.

Rumwold described an ancient, hollow stone that would be found within. A stone through which a man could travel, and which was dedicated to many things, long forgotten. He demanded this be brought.

The stone was found, just as the newborn had predicted, but of course the thing was huge, impossible for the men to carry across such treacherous ground. When the report came, Rumwold was still. Stared dead at the hut and lifted his stubby, ungrown arms. He then sent the pair of grim and wild-eyed wanderers to do the task alone.

As soon as the travelling men touched the altar it lifted, weightless, and almost floated with them across the marsh to Rumwold, who held his gaze all the while. When they arrived it crashed to earth, heavy once more, and the exhausted baby took again to his mother's breast. As he suckled, water filled the hollow of the stone.

Rumwold was baptised then, according to the rites that he instructed, meticulously. They say that in that meadow, in what today we call King's

Sutton, there the grasses neither fade nor wither, but remain always green, with the sweet scent of nectar.

The ritual complete, strict to the newborn's instructions, he sang a song of such pure, elf-strange beauty, that all there who heard it wept. Silence then reigned for much time, until he began to speak once more.

'The wisdom of a father is his son. So a father is in his son and a son in his father, and the spirit of our people is in both, and in every one.'

Rumwold told them then all truths there were to know, and spoke the Ealdspell complete, old gods and new. Told that the old must nurture and birth the new, and the new must care for and value the old. Many, many things did Rumwold tell them there, and for three days and three nights he did so, unsleeping, and all who listened were enrapt, and ever-changed.

And on the third day he finished his tale, and before their eyes they saw the tiny baby start to age, and though his frame stayed small and childlike, his skin did wrinkle, and his hair did pulse and grey and thin, and his eyes did fade.

Rumwold with a smile then told them of the hour he'd die, and did command that, on his death, he must remain where he was born for a year, then move to what today we know as Brackley for a further two. In these places would he grant health and plenty, and they would be ever rich in crops, and once the three years were paid he would rest until the crack of doom, in what today we know as Buckingham.

Rumwold's withered body shrank, then, his voice ceased, and at the hour he appointed his glory departed. Of the words he spoke almost all have since been forgotten, though fragments remain, and some I have collected here, passed on through generations.

Out of the mouth of babes.

The Hind
of Domne
Eafe

That wild Eadbald, son of Ethelbert, first of the three, took his
father's young wife to bed soon after her husband died – as
both found the arrangement pleasing, in short order a marriage
was held, and two sons born.

Eldest was Eormenred, who had four children, each blessed in birth by
the middengods Eostre and Erce – two sons (Aethelred and Aethelbert),
and two daughters (Eormengith and Eormenburh, who also was known
as Domne Eafe).

Youngest was Eorcenberht, who also had four children – again, two
sons (Egbert and Hlothhere) and two daughters.

Eorcenberht, the younger, became king when Eadbald died, and when
Eorcenberht died also, his son Egbert became king in his stead. When
Eormenred (the elder) and his wife died, his own sons, Aethelred and
Aethelbert, were still children, and so these orphans were fostered with
King Egbert, their cousin, to join his comitatus when they were of age.

The most powerful man in Egbert's court, and his closest adviser in
war, was a battle-worshipper of Thunner who had taken that high god's
name, and was known to all as Thunor.

Thunor had the task of training the boys, and he found them poor and
hopeless students. He had, in dreams, a vision of a future in which the
princes grew to weak and cowardly men, and on Egbert's death took
kingship of Kent, and unwise in war they led the land to its destruction,
and the reaving of its people.

Thunor could not allow it.

He brought his concerns to the king, described his vivid dreams, and
Egbert had pause. Thunor brought the king to watch their training, and
see their weakness in war. And Egbert had pause. Thunor told the king
they must be killed, and begged the king to leave it in his hands, to close
the door and ask no questions.

Egbert said nothing. Thunor understood.

That night the king slept, and Thunor did not.

Neither of the boys would see daylight again.

Come morning, Egbert was woken by his attendants, and told to come
quick to his hall, for strange happenings were afoot. There he saw crowds
gathering in amazement at the great beam of light that shone from the roof.

Inside, the king saw the light went through and down into the hall,
penetrating his great throne and the very floor beneath. Panicked, he

called for Thunor, and demanded to know where his cousins were.

Thunor looked at the king. Egbert asked again.

'You know full well, my lord.'

The king demanded a third time to know, on their friendship.

'They sleep in your hall, beneath your throne, deep with Mother Erce.'

The king held a witan, then, and it was agreed by all that they should send for the boys' sister, who dwelt in Mercia, explain that her brothers were dead, and determine what she would accept as weregild – blood-money, a compensation for death or disablement.

Men called her Domne Eafe – she was older than the boys, followed the Gloryfather, and had married a son of Penda named Merewalh, or Merwal, who ruled a sub-kingdom of Mercia named Magonsaete, in what today is Herefordshire and Shropshire.

Domne Eafe took the news well, and pronounced to the king that as the slain were her own brothers, so must she have the land that first was her ancestral brothers', and demanded part of the island of Thanet, where Hengest and Horsa first stepped foot.

Egbert agreed.

They travelled, then, over the River Wantsume, and when the king asked how much land she desired, there appeared an elf-white hind before them, which bowed to Domne Eafe, and held the mark of Eostre. She told the king, then, that she would take whatever land this hind would gently lead them round.

Knowing the deer would likely bolt at any moment, the king agreed, and gave his word to it. The hind then placidly guided them round and round, on and on, hour after hour, until Thunor, exasperated, ran in front and bellowed at the king, 'How long will you follow this trickery? Will you give it all away?' And he went then to grab the hind, which did not move.

As Thunor touched the white of its neck, the earth beneath him opened up and bit into his legs, and chewed and swallowed him down into itself, and as he screamed to the high gods and Thunner ignored his pleas, Thunor disappeared, and Erce the middengoddess ate her fill.

The mound that took him was thereafter known as *Thunures hleaw*.

After a brief pause, the hind continued to lead them on procession. Egbert gave the land without fuss.

The best gods, some say, are the closest ones to hand.

Snake-stone and Cattle-song

H ilda was born in AD 614. When her father was poisoned
whilst wreccan, she found herself fostered to his uncle, King
Edwin, and raised in his Northumbrian court.
It was whilst she still was a child that Coifi took her under
his wing, taught and showed her things, told of days long gone when he'd
defeated wyrms. When she laughed, he merely smiled, and pulled back his
hood. He tapped his stick upon the ground, and from where no snake had
been before, one appeared, and came towards them.

Coifi gently touched the snake with the tip of his staff. Instantly it
curled up, tight, and turned to stone. He gave the stick to Hilda, for to
try, and as he did he suddenly wasn't there, and as he did a thousand
snakes or more were writhing through the grounds, and the people
screamed, and Hilda felt the mad-craft in her. She raised that grim stick,
then, and struck the ground, and forced herself into the strike, and every
single snake that touched earth then coiled tight, and turned to stone, as
she'd been taught by Coifi.

Coifi gave her then his blessing, and led her to a life that served the
Gloryfather, just as Coifi taught her. It was he who directed her to found
the abbey at Whitby, of which only ruins remain. Thereafter, every bird
that held allegiance to Coifi gave her due respect, and whether sea eagle
or raven or other kind, as they flew past that Wada-crafted coast they'd
dip and fall to ground to pay obeisance.

Time passed, and Hilda grew old in her grim abbey.

There was a certain mead hall then, within its vicinity, at which
gathered the men of the area, amongst whom was an old one named
Caedmon. Illiterate and uneducated, Caedmon had spent his long life as
a cowherd, and still was. After a long, hard day of toil he would make his
way to the hall, enjoy ribaldry, food and drink, and then duck out before
the harp was passed around – it was customary then to pass the harp, one
man to the other, each singing a tale or song in turn, well known or made
up – something to while the hours away in social pleasure.

Caedmon hated it. He could not sing, he knew no tales, he could not
play and could not talk with eloquence or clarity. For him there was
no greater shame than to receive the harp, and then to feel the heat of
mockery from all at table as he choked and barked and croaked away.

One day, after his familiar toil, he took his seat and turned to chat to his neighbour to find the man unfamiliar. Strangers were rare, and so he asked the grim man's name. He introduced himself as Coifi.

And they talked and they talked, and time and again did Coifi pass Caedmon his mead, and time and again did Caedmon drink it, and it was sweet and good, and unlike any mead that Caedmon then before had drunk. Such fine talks did they have, and so much did this wise and travelled Coifi know to talk of, that before he knew it the harp was circling the table. Caedmon, drink-blind, feeling fire of shame in chest already, lurched to standing and bolted for the door, just in time.

Stumbling to the stables, and finding the herd assigned to him that night, he saw to food and water before folding up in a corner and falling asleep.

And as he did, he dreamed.

And in his dreams a hooded man stood by him, and hailed and greeted and addressed him by his name, 'Caedmon, sing me something.'

Caedmon felt ashamed, and said, 'I cannot sing and know no tales, and so I fled the feast.'

'Nevertheless, you must sing.'

'What must I sing?'

'Sing to me a shaping song.'

And Caedmon felt his chest to hum, and from it started flowing verses and words that he never had heard, and there sang Caedmon the Ealdspell in its entirety, in that strange land of Dream.

Caedmon bolted awake, with no idea of the time, and with the memory of all he had sung still fresh and alive within him. He spent the day in toil, and went to hall, and to table, and chatted and ate and drank, and when the harp came to him he stayed, and sang.

The hall was enrapt. All night did Caedmon sing to them then, of things they knew so well, and things they'd never heard before.

The next day, once word had spread, Hilda sought him out, had him sing to her, and wept. She gave him then a place in her monastery, and his only toil thereafter was to read and to learn all the lore she could find to teach him, and to turn it into song. He wrought many songs of the Ealdspell, and never again did meet that Coifi, but lived full eld, and told many, many tales, and won a happy death.

The Urith Sacrifice

Once upon a time, an English man and an English woman moved to the British kingdom of Dumnonia, to what we now call Stowford, in Devon. Now the line between Wessex and Devon then was blurred, and many crossed back and forth between the two, and much mingling of culture and people took place. This soon led to their melding, with Devon soon enough becoming part of Wessex, and the border of the Tamar established to divide it from Cornwall.

In time the English woman was pregnant, and in time the English woman gave birth, and though her husband gained a daughter that day, he also lost a wife.

Urith then was born in the blood of her mother.

Now these were hard and brutal times, and a man alone could not raise a newborn. He did not even know what to name her.

A local woman came to him, that night, and lay with him, and told him that the child's name was Urith, who was the mother of their people, the mother of the land.

He was a good husband to her, his new wife, and he loved her as well as he could love, but it was his daughter, Urith, who had his heart, and his dead love who would ever define it. As the years passed, his new wife grew to hate the girl for this, for the purity of love the child so casually possessed, that could never be known by her.

A time came, in these hard and brutal days, of terrible drought. Birds fell from the sky in thirst, trees withered, crops died. A terrible blight rent the land of Devonshire, and so young Urith took to her knees and she prayed, as she had been taught to. She prayed first to the Gloryfather, the god of all gods, and then to His mother, and then to her own, from whose corpse she was born.

'You are right to pray to Mother, little one.'

Urith looked up to see her stepmother standing over her.

'Come, let me take you to her.'

Now Urith had never seen the spot where her mother was buried, and so went eagerly where her stepmother led. They walked first by a dry ditch that once had been a stream.

'Is my mother here?'

'No, child, further on.'

They walked next by woodland, filled with yellowed trees.

'Is my mother here?'

'No, child, further on.'

They came finally to a field, bound by thick hedge on all sides, with dry, tall crops all about, much higher than the girl's head.

'Is my mother here?'

'Yes, child, further on.'

And her stepmother led her into the crops, and they disappeared into them, and walked to what felt like the centre, felt like a mound, the tall stalks obliterating all but the blue sky above – for the crops which grow now, which reach our hips at best, are not the crops which grew then. Corn then stood well above a man, sometimes seven foot high, and towered tall over young, maiden girls who would never walk out from amongst them.

'Call out to Mother, child.'

And Urith called out, and before her the dry crops parted and a woman stood, and in her hands was a scythe. The girl gasped and blinked. To her left the crops parted again, and another woman emerged, standing over her, scythe in hand. Behind her came another. And another. And another.

'I don't understand; where is my mother?'

'Urith, you are our mother.'

And the women who surrounded her raised their scythes and swung and reaped the head from Urith's pale, thin neck, and sowed Mother Erce, Mother Erth, Mother Urth, with the blood and the bone and the flesh of her. Where her head hit the ground, water began to flow, and the crops drank and life returned.

Where blood fed, red flowers grew, which we call scarlet pimpernel, and the well that was birthed by Urith that day flows still, in Chittlehampton, and every year runs red with the blood that she gave, to and for and from her mother, as her mother gave it to and for and from her daughter.

And Mother Erce was satisfied, and Urith returned to Urth.

The
Halgan
of the
North

At that Battle of Winwaed where Penda finally fell, a certain spear-man fought for King Oswiu, whose name was Cuthbert. He was of noble birth, and had strange talents that had won him friends amongst the warriors. Despite meagre rations, always he had meat and mead, and in battle he found himself enriched with god-strength.

Often he would speak of seeing the souls of the slain carried far from Middle Earth, sometimes by the Waelcyrge, sometimes by shining, elf-bright figures, sometimes by other things.

Standing by the River Tyne on a rough day, watching some monks in rafts get carried out to sea by angry waters as a crowd on the opposite bank laughed and jeered, Cuthbert asked his companion why they cursed the men being carried away to destruction, 'Would it not be better and more kindly to pray for their safety, rather than to rejoice over their dangers?'

Coifi pulled back his hood, and replied, 'They have robbed men of their old ways of worship, and how the new worship is to be conducted, nobody knows.'

So, with his spear and his sword, Cuthbert set off to discover how.

As he travelled he grew hungry and, seeing an eagle flying aloft, he called out, 'Erne, have you food for me?'

The eagle looked to him and nodded, and dove then to the river, catching up a large fish which he brought to Cuthbert, who took it from Erne's talons, cut it in two with his seax, and returned half to the bird. He set a fire and cooked his own, and he and the eagle dined together before Cuthbert resumed his journey.

In time, and after many adventures, he came to discover an island named Farne, which was not like the rest of the Lindisfarne region, for twice a day it was cut off from the land, and twice a day returned contiguous.

This isle in marsh and fen was no ordinary place, and none had yet dared dwell there, for it was home to orcs and to ettins, to goat-riders and other things. When Cuthbert heard of this he understood his task, and with a glint of mad-craft in his eye he took up sword and spear, and let the battle-heat within his chest seethe once again, and in grim frenzy there did Cuthbert take the island, single-handed, and with much might and slaughter the under-things were killed, or driven far away.

Cuthbert, then, was monarch of his land.

Battle-shining still, the wanderer set to building a city there, fitted for his rule. The houses he saw in Dream, and they were strange, round things, with a single, tall storey above ground and another two below, cut into the living rock, so the inhabitant could see nothing but the sky from within.

He made the wall of rough, unworked stone and turf removed from the excavations, and many said this craft could not be carried through, for it was not the way that things were done, but Cuthbert did it nonetheless, and lifted rocks, alone, of mighty weight.

To finish the rooves, he called to Hraefn, and the raven came and gathered straw and turf and placed it on the rough-hewn timber, and his kin who lived on the island joined and did likewise. For three days and three nights they toiled, and when their work was complete Hraefn brought to Cuthbert a portion of hog's lard, which thereafter he would use to grease the shoes of visitors.

Cuthbert then built up his isle, on human scale with crooked, ancient beauty, and grew to be considered strong in wisdom as he was in arm, and many visited to seek his counsel, and many wondrous acts did he perform, and he was thought a holy man, or halgan.

One monkish visitor, in particular, glimpsed things he did not understand. He watched at night as agéd Cuthbert stole from out his earthen house and walked to shore, and entered in the waters there, up to his neck, and sang songs then to Geofon, and joined with her, and spent the dark hours of the night watching and singing to the sound of the waves.

When the monk and his fellows decided it was time to leave, those same waters boiled up in rage and would not allow them. Cuthbert, unperturbed, called a goose to him, lifted and took it to the water, and with some muttered words he slit its throat and let it bleed to the tide.

He gave it to them then, told them to eat it, and all would be well.

The monks were shocked by this, and uncomfortable, and left it on a wall to hang, deciding to wait out the storm. Cuthbert smiled, and left them to their devices.

A day passed, and still the storm raged. Three days, and it was unabated. Full seven days they remained on the island, shut in by the raging seas, and Cuthbert came to them once more, and saw the goose

that hung uncooked upon the wall, and laughed and said, 'Does not the goose hang there still unconsumed? Why marvel that she does not let you leave? Put it quickly to the pot, cook and eat, that Geofon may quieten and let you go.'

They did as he commanded, and as the goose was cooked the waves calmed, and when the meal was finished, they saw the sea was placid, and went aboard their ship and, with favourable winds, returned home, with feelings both of joy and shame, confused by what they'd seen.

When old, and near to death, one morning Cuthbert found a visitor he did not know he had. Tall he was, grim-visaged, looking round approvingly at all the work which Cuthbert, the old warrior, there had done. Excited by an unexpected guest, Cuthbert welcomed him warmly, washed and cleaned his feet, and set about preparing food for him – for it was Yuletide, and no time for fasting, and the man was surely tired from his night-journey through the snow-laden winds. The hooded man refused, answering that the hall he was hastening to was very far away, and they would feast together soon.

Cuthbert insisted, placed a table with food before him, and went to fetch freshly baked bread. When he returned he could not find the guest whom he had left eating, yet the snow-covered earth showed no footsteps from the table.

Instead, piled high, were three hot loaves, elf-white and excellent. Loaves such as the Middle Earth cannot produce, which surpass the lily in whiteness, the rose in fragrance, and honey in taste. There was only one hall Cuthbert knew of where such bread was served.

He smiled, then, as Penda had before him, bid his island goodbye, and returned to his cell to wait for death.

For he was not confused by what he'd seen.

The
Evengloom
of the
Gods

In forests and on islands, things last longer than in cities and towns. So, too, in the Juten territories of the Ytene Forest and the Isle of Wight, the old ways lasted longer than anywhere else. The Wight had its own royal line, and in all of England and out of all of England's kings, the very last to hold Woden over the Allruler was a king of the island, a King of the Wihtwara.

King Arwald was a descendant of Wihtgar, and King Caedwalla of Wessex a descendant of Cerdic. Where once their ancestors had ruled as friends and kinsmen, these distant cousins now were enemies; where Arwald clung unstinting to the worship of their greatest grandfather, Caedwalla embraced the tools of this new Christianity for as long as it served him, and wielded the hammer and tongs of religion to forge his own greedy ends (Caedwalla, bear in mind, was not baptised – far too permanent a commitment to something so flighty as a god).

For Caedwalla had a hunger in him, a hunger that gnawed and chewed and whispered always for more, and this hunger it was that caused him to demand the land of the heathen Arwald, to praise this brand-new Christ that still was strange to cruel Caedwalla's tongue.

The Island was and is small, with only around thirty extended families living there in Arwald's time. When Caedwalla's hungry men arrived, the waves of them crashed against the Wihtwara like salt-water wearing away the cliffs, eroding hope and overwhelming all resistance.

The butchery and slaughter that overcame the island scarred the land and gouged its mark in memory; its inhabitants were all but utterly destroyed, with those who refused to convert killed mercilessly and publicly, their lands and their possessions divvied up amongst the gleeful conquerors.

Arwald was dead; maimed, executed and left as a message. The day and the island were lost. Chaos reigned, and from this chaos, from this panic, two brothers fled.

Now these were noble brothers, for their closest kin (some say father, some say sibling) had until very recently been that same Arwald, king, though little enough of their royal bearing was now on display. Frightened, they were, and desperate on the day they galloped from Arwald's falling army, but gallop they did, on and on, past burning house and blackened tree, until they reached the cliffs, and the shore, and the ferryman.

'Safe passage for two!' called the elder.

'Safety's hard to come by these days, and rarely had cheap.'

The ferryman was wrinkled, long-bearded and stooped; a grey hood hid half his face, a single, tired eye on show, gazing at and through them.

'Just get us to the mainland.' The younger shoved a pouch, tight with coins, into the ferryman's hands: 'And there's for your silence.'

The ferryman nodded, and set to his task as the brothers leapt aboard, watching the terror of what remained on the island recede. They sat in near silence then. As the ferryman rowed they watched him row, and as the ferryman rowed they stared into the mists, and as the ferryman rowed they whispered soft, urgent prayers to the old gods beneath their breath.

'Words are worth little, on days such as these.'

The brothers looked back to the grim old man.

'What do you mean?' asked the elder.

'Just as I say,' the ferryman rumbled from deep within his grey hood, rowing out a steady, even pace through the mist.

'Just get us to the other side. It's not your counsel that we seek,' said the younger with a glare.

The grim ferryman nodded, and the silence returned.

Above them the sky thundered and the clouds brewed dark, raven and eagle circling high. Around them the mists grew thick. Behind them wolves howled and heathens screamed.

After days or hours, minutes or seconds, from the deep of the mist rose the land that they sought – the Ytene.

The brothers disembarked, knowing they had precious little time before their absence was noted and search parties sent.

'Thanks be to you, grandfather!' the elder called as the ferryman began to depart once more.

'Speak not of what you've seen here today!' the younger added sharply.

The grim old ferryman looked to them both, as his boat started wearily to drift back the way it had come, back into the mist.

'Words are worth little, on days such as these.'

They pressed on, deep into the Ytene. After a time they came to a great clearing, in which the moon shone full well, and the great sky seemed to magnify, and the stars stare down. In the clearing sat an old, old goat of a man, older even than the ferryman, with deep and faded scars, ancient, dented, rusted armour and a broken blade by his side. By the time they noticed, he was already gazing full at them, with the endless blue of his endless eyes. The elder spoke first.

'Hail, stranger.'

'Strange days, indeed,' the old man whispered, his face bright in the starlight, one arm hidden by his side, 'yet I know you two well enough.'

'And who are you, that should know us so well?' the younger threw back.

'Just an old soldier, who isn't now what once he was.'

'And who do you know us to be?' the elder asked.

'Brothers, good and true. If it's aid you want, and shelter, I shall give.'

The younger whispered sharply to his brother: 'An old fool, he'll betray us for a bath. We should kill him.'

The elder looked square at his brother, before turning back to the old soldier.

'Thank you, but you are mistaken, I think. Good night, friend.'

He carried on his way, the younger following quickly after, but not before a whispered threat behind: 'Speak not of what you've seen tonight!'

The old soldier sat alone in the shade of the clearing, watched after their absence, the North Star shining bright in the scars and the lines of his old and weathered face.

'Words are worth little, on days such as these.'

The brothers pressed on, deep into the Ytene. After some time the crash and thunder of the storm returned, intensified, and they came to a dense thicket of woodland, in which a huge, broad ox of a man chopped wood from an oak in time to the storm, with a bright, hot axe. By the time they noticed, he was already gazing full at them. The elder spoke first.

'Hail, stranger.'

'Strange days, indeed,' the large man bellowed, 'yet I know you two well enough.'

'And who are you, that should know us so well?' the younger threw back.

'Just an axeman and a forester, doing what I can.'

'And who do you know us to be?' the elder asked.

'Brothers, good and true. If it's aid you want, and shelter, I shall give.'

The younger whispered sharply to his brother: 'A young buck, he'll betray us for a title. We should kill him.'

The elder looked square at his brother, before turning back to the woodsman.

'Thank you, but you are mistaken, I think. Good night, friend.'

And he carried on his way, the younger following quickly after, but not before a whispered plea behind: 'Speak not of what you've seen tonight!'

The large man returned to his axe, splitting wood with every roll of storm. He called after them without looking, knowing his great, booming voice would find their ears.

'Words are worth little, on days such as these!'

The brothers pressed on, deep into the Ytene. Soon the storm calmed and quieted, and by and by they came to a hunting lodge, and next to it a tall and twisted tree, blackened and dark, and by it stood a fat and well-dressed man. By the time they noticed, he was already gazing full at them. The elder spoke first.

'Hail, stranger.'

'Strange days, indeed,' the wealthy man crowed, peering at them both, 'yet I know you two well.'

'And who are you, that should know us so well?' the younger threw back.

'An Ealdorman here, and great friend to you.'

'And who do you know us to be?' the elder asked.

'Kin to King Arwald, good and faithful. I have long been ally to your noble line, and would consider it an honour, if it's aid you want and shelter, to give you both forthwith. Such fair and highborn men should not be out on so foul a night as this.'

The elder muttered to the younger, 'I do not know this man. We should press on.'

The younger looked square at his brother, before turning back to the Ealdorman.

'We thank you, sir, and would be honoured to accept your hospitality. We have travelled far, and our enemies are vast.' The Ealdorman dropped to his knee.

'The honour, lordlings, is entirely mine. Come, take shelter in my lodge and I shall send for food and drink befitting of such highborn guests. You may be assured of my aid, and I do swear no enemy shall find you here.' With a flourish he rose and entered the lodge, the younger following quickly after. The elder paused a pace before joining them, glancing at the dark tree. He shut the heavy door tight behind them.

Inside the lodge the Ealdorman spared no expense. A great table sat, which soon enough was filled with cooked meats, rich fruits and fine bread. Ale and mead and wine was brought and shared, songs were sung by warmth of fire, and the three drank and laughed and told each other tales of that great Arwald, shared old stories of old gods and long-forgotten heroes; of Badda and of Gefwulf, of Hringweald and Seaxneat. Soon the brothers were full of belly, warm of heart, and peaceful of mind.

The strong and friendly ale sent them happy, happy dreams. The brothers slept, a deep and peaceful sleep.

When they woke it was roughly, and to an armed guard.

The Ealdorman was nowhere to be seen.

'Treacherous wyrm!' cursed the younger.

The elder remained quiet.

The brothers were dragged from the lodge and into a small clearing, their hands bound behind them. Pushed to their knees, the soldiers circled, raising sword and spear. From behind the ranks, two men entered: the unbaptised Caedwalla, and the Christian missionary Wilfred.

'Convert or die.'

After a pause that lasted a lifetime, Caedwalla repeated himself.

'Convert or die.'

'Life,' whispered the younger.

'Louder.'

'Please, let us live,' the younger begged. The elder remained speechless, his mind elsewhere.

Wilfred went about the ritual, and under the gaze of swords, the brothers were christened. Caedwalla bid them stand, wrists still bound.

'Arwald's heirs. The old fox might have held out, but Wihtwara's baptised now. Kill them.'

With quick flick of blade the younger's throat was opened, and he dropped with a throttled gasp to his knees, and fell lifeless to a penitent bow, blood pooling from the jarred neck, life flowing to the forest floor.

The elder moved like lightning, headbutted the nearest man, stamped hard as heaven-fire to the side of the knee and heard the crack of bone-locks burst. As the spearmen shot forward the elder forced his strength to his legs, gave a final great cry, 'To Woden!'

He hurled himself backwards, momentum and bodyweight driving against the pointed limb of the tree behind, impaling him upright, hanging from the branches. By the time the spears had nailed his body further to the wood, he had already died on his feet.

The brothers were buried there, where they had died, and the New Forest took their meat as food. Caedwalla returned to the boats, and was rowed back to the conquered island. As the Ytene began to recede, further down the shore he watched an old, hooded ferryman greet two figures in the distance. One boarded, the other remained behind, and the vessel disappeared into mist. The last thing of the land to be lost to sight, as Caedwalla drifted further, was the lone figure of the one who remained, staring out to sea, searching for the ferryman who would not take him.

There are some who tell it different. How the brothers after capture were happily baptised in a chapel at Stoneham, and willingly submitting to execution the next day, confident of their place in a Christian heaven. As Caedwalla, their killer, was still un-christened, this made the brothers martyrs, and they're known by some today as the dual Christian saint, St Arwald, named for their defeated, pagan father or brother.

There are others still who say the ferryman was seen again by Caedwalla. That for his slaughter the old gods hounded him, and soon he could not eat or sleep or ride without them flooding all his senses. Soon enough he fled the land of Woden, desperate to be free from English gods, and sailed to Rome to be baptised; it takes a god to beat a god.

Every day of the journey he watched the vague and shadowy shape of a grim, hooded ferryman far behind, following at a distance just within and just beyond the bounds of sight. Caedwalla arrived in Rome, and still he was pursued. Caedwalla had his baptism, and still he was pursued. Ten days after Caedwalla was christened, in the 689th year of his Lord, Caedwalla was found dead.

Some say that Woden took him. Some say that it was Christ. Some say the younger brother's ghost still walks the New Forest, chained to his remains, or watches lonely from the shore for the ferryman who one day might take him, on to find some peace.

Some, who worship still the old gods, praise Arwald now as triple saint; the younger, the elder, the king – the False, the Redeemed, and the True. Some say that on Arwald's feast day, April 22nd, the ferryman returns to shore where the younger waits, and with him are the elder and the king, and the four return to where the two were killed, where a great table sits, filled with cooked meats, rich fruits and fine bread. Mead is shared, songs sung by warmth of fire, and the four drink and laugh and tell each other tales of old, old gods and long-forgotten men.

Some say a great many things, but words are worth little, on days such as these.

Osgyth and the Stag

This story starts, once more, with a child of Penda.

Wilburga married Frithuwold when still he held to the old way – a sub-king in Mercia, ruling over what we now call Surrey. In time, of course, both came to hold the Allruler highest, and when they had a daughter of their own, at Quarrendon, near Aylesbury, this daughter was named Osgyth, and raised to know the Gloryfather as her own, and nothing more of any other.

But gods are things of habit, and it's a rare god indeed who reacts to change with warmth.

The sight and presence of this fresh child, with such Wodenish descent, raised without knowledge of her foregods, was an insult. Those still quick to rage took umbrage at it, and few rage faster or harder than that middenmistress of the seas.

So it was, one day, that Osgyth's aunt, Edith (who should have known better), sent her on an errand to take a book of Christian thought to her other aunt, Modwenna. The route she wandered crossed a stream, which – as you know and she didn't – was the domain of Geofon. As Osgyth crossed the bridge without a by-your-leave, and bore that book that sought to unwrite ancient lore, Geofon raised the waters there into a great and grasping hand, which gripped and crushed young Osgyth into itself, raised her high and dashed her low to the wet.

Three days passed.

When Edith eventually travelled herself to Modwenna, she found that Osgyth had never arrived. The women set out searching for her, then, and as they traced the steps and saw the stream they realised their mistake, and rushing to its banks and looking down they saw, still gripped tight at the bottom of the bed, the bloated corpse of their once-niece, the book still in her hands.

The women pleaded then with Geofon to release the girl, to no avail.

They pleaded then to the water itself, and to the Gloryfather above.

Finally, as a grim-faced, hooded traveller crossed the bridge, so Geofon gave up her prize, flung Osgyth back to Erce, and took the waters of death from out her lungs.

Osgyth breathed her life once more.

But Geofon can hold a grudge, and Geofon seethed at this. She felt through her domain then, until she found a corner of the country where

she could work her wiles and, dripping moist in watery curves, appeared before one Sighere, who held joint kingship of Essex with his kinsman Saebbi. Both held to the Gloryfather then, but men are weak, and the briny joys of Geofon seductive. She lured him with her watery delights, for which he agreed to give her dominion over his first-born child.

When Geofon instructed him to seek a wife, and to seek the hand of the daughter of Frithuwold and Wilburga, he all too happily agreed. Frithuwold and Wilburga, in turn, accepted the match on their daughter's behalf, oblivious to all.

When Osgyth returned to her parents, she found the wedding planned. In short order the swords and the rings were swapped, the oaths were made, the feasts were feasted upon, and they were husband and wife and bound for London, then capital of the kingdom of Essex.

That night, Geofon tickled about Sighere, and used her wiles to stoke his fire, and set him in hot mood to take his bride within their marital bed, and fill her with a plumpened child.

Osgyth knew that something was wrong.

She played along, however, suggesting that they drink and revel first, and this they did, and Osgyth mixed her husband's drinks in such a way that flesh soon failed him, and he passed out unsatisfied, and Geofon's frustration grew.

Next night, Geofon once more spurred Sighere on, and set him in hot mood, and Osgyth played along, suggesting that they feast and revel first, and this they did, and Osgyth mixed her husband's foods in such a way that they rebelled, and he remained unsatisfied, and Geofon's frustration grew.

The third night came, and Sighere then would not take food or drink, and Osgyth feigned a deathly headache, and Sighere gruffly did concede, remaining still unsatisfied, and Geofon's frustration hit its peak, and she would not allow delay.

When Osgyth woke she woke to Sighere close to her, and though he did not hold the Gloryfather high, his body had grown strong in battle, and he was mighty, and his touch felt hot and good, and his eyes were deep and fine, and his lips were warm and wet.

And just as Osgyth found her fires stoked, from what felt far and far away she heard a muffled voice, and suddenly her husband was not with her, and instead was at the window calling back, rushing to get clothes about his taught and sweating body.

As Osgyth looked outside, she saw there something she had never seen – just past the gate there stood a huge and spreading elf-white stag, grim-visaged, many-pointed, and about its neck there was a crown, of a sort that was not seen in England. The king then kissed his wife and promised they would finish this anon, then ran to join his men in hunt, and as they did the stag did run, and led them on a merry chase round and about, for days and days on end.

By the time the king returned, he found his wife remarried.

Osgyth had become a nun.

In frustration at losing both of his quarries, Sighere then rejected Geofon, returned to worship of the Gloryfather, and granted his ex-wife an estate at Chich, where she built a priory that still bears her name.

Geofon then raged.

Twice she had been thwarted.

She stretched herself across her bed beneath the waves, then, and searched, and after many years she found the perfect vessel on her surface, filled with reavers and with raiders, and she caressed the boat and called to those aboard, and promised them all that they could hope to want if they would serve her, and with the fires of their hunger burning about the ship, she carried them eager to Osgyth's monastery.

They came from the mere, and they overwhelmed. Dragged Osgyth to the shore, and beheaded her on the tide, as sacrifice to Geofon.

As axe hurled through throat her head flew high, and high, and danced on wind and soared inshore, away from Geofon, and where it landed flowed strange healing waters which that goddess had no power over, and Osgyth's headless body picked itself up and walked away from the waves, and walked to the fresh and bubbling spring, took up her head and carried it to her church, staining the door with still-flowing blood.

Her body was found in prayer, and is still there somewhere today, enshrined. Her ghost can still be seen at twilight, riding a great and elf-white stag about the bounds of her land.

Geofon was bested that day, and took her anger out on the followers who had failed her. As they tried to sail away the waters went dead still, and the flames of their hunger were stoked beyond hunger, and the blaze erupted from them, and the vessel was consumed.

The fire in the water took all.

For many generations thereafter, those living at the priory, when they went to bed, did rake up the fire in the hearth, and make the shape of an X in the ashes, and pray to Osgyth to deliver them from fire, and from water, and from all other ancient misadventure.

There are some who say, within that priory, that ever since has Geofron been spoken of in hushed, respectful tones, and that the dwellers there still soothe her, and sate her enmity as Osgyth did. Some others say that she and Eostre and Erce are three and one at once, a trinity of their own; some call these middengoddesses the Mothers, and honour them on Christmas Eve, deep in the depths of Yule.

There are those, too, who say that on the Middle Earth today these middenmothers have a power greater than the high, and never waned, though many disagree.

Still others claim that they have seen, there in the priory, a grim and hooded figure bent, perhaps in prayer to Osgyth, working mad-craft through the night for ends beyond the ken of man, as outside waves crash, screaming.

They rake up the fire in the hearth, then, make the shape of an X in the ash, and hope beyond hope to see morning.

The Vision of Dryhthelm

Once upon a time, in the kingdom of Northumbria, at a place today named Cunningham, there lived a comfortable man, richer than most though not as rich as many, with a comfortable wife and comfortable children.

His comfort was built on the comfort he was born to, and his life had been lived for himself, casting off the old fashions of his forefathers, leaving his children to their own devices, and focusing on his immediate needs; his own life, his own comforts. Old he grew, but still he would not give what he had been given, and would not gift his children as his father had gifted him, for it would mean he went without.

One day, Dryhthelm died.

His family were sad, and were relieved. His children now could start their lives, and raise their sons and daughters in stability. All night they sat then with the corpse in vigil, forgiving him his sins and remembering fondest memories, smiling generously over less fond ones, and trying hard to not remember nasty ones at all.

As the sun rose, and the cock crowed, the corpse opened its eyes and screamed. Dryhthelm's children screamed, and Dryhthelm's dog screamed, and Dryhthelm's wife screamed, rooted to the spot as the rest fled.

Dryhthelm stopped screaming, blinked, looked at his trembling wife and said: 'You'll never guess where I've been.'

Dryhthelm told her then a tale.

* * *

As he had lain there, fast in his dead body, and watched and heard all, above him stood a tall and shining elf-white figure. He took Dryhthelm by the hand, lifted him from his body and led him silently away, through places he'd not noticed before, past things that he had always and never seen.

After days or hours or seconds or years, they came to somewhere not the Middle Earth.

On and on stretched this strange, divided land, and Dryhthelm stood with his guide at the centre of a vale of great breadth and depth, and infinite length. On either side of the valley yawned two sides of this low world – all flame and heat and burning on one, all ice and spite and harrowing snow on the other.

Each side alike was filled with screaming people, each blinded to all but themselves, each deaf to all pain but their own; all in constant motion, running about one terrible landscape, then hurling themselves high above into the other. Above the vale these wretches flew in both directions, endlessly, back and forth – for those that burned were desperate for the cold, and those that froze were desperate for the heat, and each extreme was overwhelming.

Dryhthelm stared at this horror, and felt the insensible heat on one side and the gibbering ice on the other, and thought he must be in the torturous realm of Helle's dungeon, and as the thought crept through his chest the one who led him turned and looked him in the eye.

'Do not believe so. This is not the pit of Helle that you imagine.'

And on they went, and as they walked a seeming cloud of darkness spread, until they were engulfed in thick, black ever-night, and on they walked, and all that Dryhthelm could see was the white of the one who led him, and on, until within the darkness Dryhthelm noticed something darker still, and just as brighter lights illuminate the day, these deeper blacks showed in the shades of night, and soon he realised that these deeper blacks were flames of cold, black flames, in great and swollen globes, rising from the pit that echoed far below, rising to a height above then falling back again into abyss. As he stared he realised with horror that each globe was filled with people, who, like sparks flying up with smoke, were tossed and thrown hither and yon, and then, with the great globe of icy flame, plummeted back down to the pain of the chasm.

As he realised what he saw the stench overcame him, and Dryhthelm fell to his knees and gasped, and the horror of it choked, and when he looked up he was alone, and the shining one was not to be seen, and his solitude towered in the stinking black, and his screaming was lost, and he cowered there hopeless and afraid.

Until he heard something behind him.

And Dryhthelm clutched his throat, immovable with fear, and the noise grew, and became terror and lamentation – hoarse screaming of hopelessness, and the cruel laughter of the mob, of the madness of crowds.

As the noise grew closer it grew plainer, and Dryhthelm saw a sprawl of twisted figures, of orcneas and ettins, cackling and jabbering to themselves. They dragged alongside them the forms of men into the midst of darkness, whilst they whooped and burbled in rapture and relish at the agony they inflicted.

Those they dragged were gurning in their fear, tearing at their skin, animal in their pleading. On they went, and the orcneas and the ettins dragged them down, down into the midst of the burning cold, through and into the Wyrmsele, and as they did the echoing sounds they made mingled into one, and soon Dryhthelm could not distinguish where the screaming of the humans ended, and the laughter of the monsters began.

As he hunched there, weeping and afraid, he heard the braying of a single, angry voice, and when he looked he saw, deep down and far away in the pit, a single orc enraged, and black flame dribbled from his mouth, from nostril and from eye, and the pitch of his scream intensified, and Dryhthelm realised that the orc was pointing at him.

All about the darkness shifted, and all that had been icy flame was orc and ettin and terror, and with inhuman speed they jerked and were about him, and the crush of it was unbearable, and in their hands and claws and stumps they held strange implements and tools, hammers and tongs and other, crueller things, but though they screamed and crushed and threatened, none took him.

At the height and pitch of this confusion, there appeared behind him the brightness of a star descending from a height beyond height, and that which it touched it purified, and that which could not be purified it drove away, and this light was Earendil, and soon the one who had led Dryhthelm returned, and took him onward and away, and on and on, until they left that world behind.

Soon before them stood a vast wall, boundless in height and length in all directions, and they walked towards it, and though no doorway or window could be seen, closer and closer they came. Just as Dryhthelm felt he could touch the rough stone, somehow they were atop the wall, and there below and far beyond stretched gentle, rolling hills – the green fields of a blissful, unknown shire, a shire that felt like childhood, or the memory of a childhood that never was.

All about was peace and quiet and good-tilled earth. The horrors of the furnace were forgotten.

Around and about this perfect shire, where the light was brighter than the brightest day, were groups of happy, well-fed men and women dressed in rough-spun white, and there was laughter and merriment, singing and music, pleasure and ease. As Dryhthelm was led through these happy bands he felt the pure and jolly glee of the countryfolk, and he wondered whether this was paradise. As the thought crept through his chest the shining, elf-bright one who led him turned and looked him in the eye.

'Do not believe so. This is not Neorxnawang as you imagine.'

On they went, and on and on, past rushing stream and babbling brook, past fat and lazy ponies, fat and lazy cows, through fields of high, tall barley and wheat, under hill and over dale, on they went, and on and on, and through a merrie woodland then they found a perfect, clean and happy light, more beautiful than Dryhthelm had conceived of beauty being.

From deep within that light a fragrance spread like incense, and otherworldly music came, and blissful singing, and so beautiful it was that all the humble glory of the shire they'd travelled through seemed nothing by comparison, and Dryhthelm bathed in that which glowed before him, and after what could have been eternity or might have been an instant, the elf-bright wanderer led him away, back the way that they had come, to the shire of green fields and rustic simplicity.

Ingui looked at Dryhthelm, as they stood amongst the happy ones.

'Do you understand all you have seen?'

As Dryhthelm tried to answer, he felt a shift, and felt the ache and pain of Middle Earth returning, and felt his body drag him down, and as he tried to hold to the pleasures of this other shire he screamed, and screamed, and woke.

* * *

Dryhthelm finished his tale, then, held his wife and his children and his grandchildren close, and told them that he loved them. Forthwith, he gave them all he had to give, and passed on all he should have long ago.

He went then to a monastery at Melrose, and lived out his days in good works there, and spoke sometimes of things he'd seen.

The rooms that he was given at the monastery lay on the bank of the River Tweed, and he could often be seen in the depths of Yuletide, and the coldest of weathers, deep amongst the icy waters, washing himself or saying prayers. When he came to shore he never removed his sodden, frozen clothes, and when he had to break the ice to bathe he did, and stood amongst it, oblivious.

When those who beheld him said, 'It is wonderful, Brother Dryhthelm, that you are able to endure such violent cold,' he simply answered –

'I have seen colder.'

In a Hole
in the
Ground

In a hole in the ground there lived a hermit. Not a narrow, deep, miners' hole, filled with seams and ores and broken tools, nor yet a stony, yawning, cavernous hole with no one in it to oppress or demean: it was a hermit-hole, and that means discomfort.

Guthlac had grown up shaped by the sagas and tales of the Ealdspell, and most especially by those of his great ancestors. He was a direct descendant of Offa and of Icel, and a collateral descendant of Penda. A mighty brood indeed. He could even claim descent from Godwine, son of the age-old Guthlac, celebrated in the songs of the ancients.

'Guthlac' literally means battle-play, and as he grew in body and in strength, our man lived up to his name, and a noble desire for command burned hot within his breast. He remembered well the valiant deeds of heroes of old, and when he turned from a boy to a man, it was to him like waking from sleep. Gathering bands of followers, then, he soon took up arms and turned wreccan, searching for adventure, the greatest that there was.

After nine years of fierceness and war-might, in which he held Hretha ever close, warming his bed nightly, he found his triumphs total and adventures spent, and with his enemies slain he set to keeping the peace. There was no man or woman who could best our mighty Guthlac in combat, and our mighty Guthlac knew it. He had fame and glory and riches, and wanted for nothing.

Which is why he could not understand his anguish.

And so, as Guthlac's mind was storm-tossed amidst the uncertain events of passing years, amidst the gloomy clouds of life's darkness, and amidst the whirling waves of the world, he abandoned his weary limbs one night to their accustomed rest.

Suddenly, he sat bolt upright in his bed.

As a wave crashing to earth, Guthlac there understood that all the sagas end in death. That Heremod died in infamy, and Beowulf's gold was worthless once it was won. When he contemplated the wretched ends of ancient kings, the fleeting riches of the world, and the contemptible glory of this temporal life, in imagination the form of his own death revealed itself to him. He realised that every day he lived took him closer to it.

Guthlac got out of his rich, warm bed, left Hretha spreading herself there, and at the age of twenty-four turned wreccan once more.

On he wandered, then, sleepless and alone, for much time and through many adventures, until finally Wyrd lead him to the great riddler named Tatwine, who told him of an island in remote and hidden parts of the fens – many had attempted to dwell there and failed, for terror of its ettins and night-stalking horrors – there might Guthlac meet, he promised, with his greatest adventure, if he had wit to find it.

Guthlac set off, through trackless bog and dismal marsh, for Crowland.

Within the centre of the island, there stood an ancient barrow-mound, built of clods of earth that greedy-comers to the waste had dug open, in the hope of finding treasure there. Through this gaping hole there seemed to be a deeper, caverned hollow, and in this hermit-hole did Guthlac make his home.

From thereon in he wore no shoes or clothes, but only animal skins, draped about him like a wodwose, or wild man. He barely ate, but dwelt within his barrow and thought, and dreamed, and starved himself, and sought the deeper lore that could explain the riddle of his life, and guide him to the great adventure which would satisfy it.

And Guthlac did despair in *uhtceare*, the sorrow before dawn, and often doubted his path, but did not let these feeling rule him.

One day, well ensconced within his hermit-hole, it felt of a sudden that the whole island trembled, in tremendous clamour. For an instant all was quiet and still, and then came again the wild cacophony of a herd of beasts, rushing together and charging his barrow with a mighty shaking of earth. All about him then were white and ragged colts, black hounds, hogs, headless bears, wyrm and wolf, and boar and stag and ox, all roaring as the raven croaked, and as they tore about him Guthlac simply closed his eyes and went inside himself, and sought the door to elsewhere.

When he opened them again, he saw the pixies and the elf-kin watching him, in different guise of small and withered, pale and strange old men, and as he watched them back they grew afeared, and travelled through the barrow-door to Elf-land, or Fairy, and bolted it shut from the other side.

Guthlac travelled then to Dream, and ever sought the deeper lore that might explain his life, and guide him to the great adventure which would satisfy it.

The next night, deep within his barrow, Guthlac was visited once more. The doorway to the Low Earth burst asunder, and they approached from

every quarter, through floor-holes and crannies, from the earth and sky, and the orcneas and the ettins were ferocious in appearance, terrible in shape, with great heads and long necks, filthy beards and shaggy ears, wild foreheads, fierce eyes, foul mouths with thick lips and horses' teeth, throats vomiting flames from twisted jaws, strident voices, raucous cries, spreading mouths and fat cheeks, pigeon breasts, scabby thighs and knotted knees on crooked, swollen stems.

With mighty and discordant shriek, they attacked and burst into his hermit-hole, and quicker than words they bound his legs and arms and took him, plunged him into the muddy waters of the black marsh beyond, beating him with iron whips and tearing at his limbs.

Guthlac simply closed his eyes and went inside himself, and this enraged the low-things further. They raised him from the waters, then, began to drag him through the freezing skies to the beating of their awful wings, carried Guthlac from the Middle Earth, and out beyond the World Tree, and down, down to the Low Earth, to the Weargen mouth of Helle.

When he beheld the smoking jaws and hot breath of that great, endless wolf, and through them saw the caverns of ice and of fire, he forgot all the torments he'd endured, and watched the sulphurous eddies of flame and frost seem almost to touch the stars with drops of spray, and orc and ettin running round the black caverns and gloomy abysses, torturing the dead with pain beyond imagining.

The horrors then told Guthlac he must enter with them, and be theirs, and Guthlac kept his eyes wide, but went inside himself, and travelled to another place they could not reach, and from that distance spoke to them and said, 'Woe unto you, who are but dust and ashes. If it is so, I am ready. Why utter empty threats from lying throats?'

Seo Helle, then, naked and resplendent in her skinless body both of charcoal and of ice, then rose and sent the creatures scattering, and Guthlac then was gripped, dragged down, down, down through vale between the ice and fire, and through a hidden doorway, and then was back inside his hermit-hole, and the door to the Low Earth bolted from the other side.

Guthlac travelled then to Dream, and ever sought the deeper lore that might explain the riddle of his life, and guide him to the great adventure which would satisfy it.

The next morning, Guthlac woke and walked from out his hermit-hole, and from the sky there fell two men. One shone, elf-bright, the other was grim-visaged, with wild countenance.

'We have tried you,' they said, 'and have tested your mod. We have tried your unconquerable heart. We have taken up against you weapons and wiles of many-colours. You have triumphed in all, and now we shall instruct you in the deeper lore, speak past and through the Ealdspell, to that which dwells beneath.'

The three returned to the barrow, then, and unlocked the door to High Earth.

Guthlac, in his animal skins and hermit-hole amongst the haunted marshes, felt his mind grow beyond the world, and there became the wisest in the Middle Earth.

Many came to him for counsel, thereafter. That King Aethelbald, who brought Mercia to its highest might, would tell of visiting the man whilst he was still in exile. As the prince bore his fears to the hermit, Guthlac smiled, leant close, and told him in perfect detail what his life contained, and told him of his Wyrd, and how he best might wear it.

Each night and every morning, then, did Guthlac welcome in these two strange visitors, and Ingui and Woden would sit there in his barrow, and they would talk of many things, and delve beneath the Ealdspell together. Woden taught the only lore that mattered, which was of sacrifice. He spoke of how to live beyond oneself, and the god who sacrificed himself to himself, explained how sacrificing gods to gods would bring about most unexpected ends, in futures far-flung, which only he could see. Guthlac smiled the grin of Penda, then, and understood.

When Guthlac died, the island burst in brightness and in light, burning from his barrow-home. The beacon could be seen for miles around, and a tower of fire stretched out beyond the Middle Earth. The air thundered in song, and smelled of nectar.

There passed from Middle Earth the best man between the seas, they say, of those whom we have ever heard created from the tribe that is the English. Mainstay of the weary, joy of kinsmen, shield of friends, on to the splendour of the light, to seek the dwellings of his homeland on the upward road. His final lesson learned, and his first about to begin.

The greatest adventure, after all, is what lies ahead.

Index

Acknowledgements

There are, of course, countless people to acknowledge and to thank for their aid and influence in writing this book, not least J.R.R Tolkien, Geoffrey of Monmouth, and the Venerable Bede. Foremost is Sally Stratford, for everything, always. There's my darling Laura Jane Romer-Ormiston, for much she knows about and much more that she doesn't. There're the lads: Alexander Larman, Matthew Nicholas, Darcy Alexander Corstorphine, William Ashcroft, Tim Grieveson, Gordon Moore, James Carney Thompson, and Geordie Naylor-Leyland. The lasses: Hesper Stratford, Jenny Stratford, and Nori. There's Peter Brice and Graham Stratford, who taught me how to be a man, and gave me so much more besides. There's Nick Hennessey, Giles Abbott, Justin Hardy, Francis Magee, John Hurt, and Jim Henson's The StoryTeller. I'd like to thank the long-forgotten zines that first published early versions of the Beginning of Wonders and the Evengloom of the Gods, and, of course, I'd like to thank Batsford and all who sail in her – Lilly Phelan, especially, for putting up with my endless pedantry, my copious revisions, and the many extended deadlines; Gemma Doyle, for designing the beautiful object you hold in your hands; Jesús Sotés, for reversing heads and adding swords long after he was contractually obliged to. Lastly, I'd like to thank you, for reading this. I really do hope you've enjoyed it, and I really do hope you retell and rewrite the stories you've found within. They belong to you, now. Do something with them.